SAVIANA STANESCU:

THE NEW YORK PLAYS

(Waxing West, Lenin's Shoe,
Aliens with Extraordinary Skills)

NoPassport Press

Dreaming the Americas Series

Saviana Stanescu: The New York Plays

Cover photo from *Aliens with Extraordinary Skills* at Women's Project, NY. Photo credit: Carol Rosegg.

NoPassport Press Dreaming the Americas Series

First edition 2010 by NoPassport Press

PO Box 1786, South Gate, CA 90280 USA; -

NoPassportPress@aol.com;

ISBN: 978-0-578-04942-7

Contents

INTRODUCTION

A Writer in R/evolution

Saviana Stanescu arrived in New York two weeks before 9/11. An award-winning journalist, poet and dramatist, who took part in the Romanian Revolution of 1989 that had brought a corrupt and brutal dictatorship to its knees, Saviana was a leader of the post-revolutionary movement that celebrated through art Romania's emerging democracy and open society. Thanks to a Fulbright Program grant, she came to the United States to study the relationship between America's theater and its successful democratic institutions; free speech, for example, was a principle for which she had fought hard in her own country. Then, within days of her arrival, she saw the United States confront the limitations of its own freedom and security. Saviana had ventured to America as an outsider in search of new ways to see the world and had gotten more than what she bargained for: a front row seat to witness America's shock and anger at its own vulnerability at Ground Zero.

As time passed, the events of 9/11 began to profoundly impact nearly everyone and everything in the United States. Because of how she had experienced social and political change in Romania, Saviana understood the ramifications of 9/11 more quickly than most Americans did. She immediately recognized the schizophrenia of power and powerlessness that manifested itself as the United States sought to redefine its role in an unstable world—a tension that was already a primary subject in her own writing in the aftermath of communism. Accustomed as she was to social and political uncertainty as a way of life, she soon felt as much an insider as an outsider. Perhaps this different way of seeing and writing about the meaning of freedom and democracy from her fresh vantage point in New York City made it possible for Saviana to begin to think of herself as an immigrant in America. The three plays in this volume, written between 2002 and 2009, chart Saviana's investigation of how her two worlds connect, and how they continue to evolve. This task is the perennial quest of the immigrant writer, of course; Saviana arrived here, however, when the idea of globalism was being newly minted, and, by studying these New York plays, we can see both how she assimilated into this country and how she held onto her global identity. We may even discover for ourselves, through the progression of her work, what it means to be an individual, an American and a global citizen in the 21st century.

Certainly the years I have spent with Saviana since 2001, when we were first introduced by Michael Johnson-Chase (who initially established the Lark Play Development Center's international program and translation initiatives), have opened my eyes to the world and inspired me to reconsider my responsibilities as both a theater maker and an American citizen. Before the Revolution of 1989 which toppled communism in Romania, Saviana informs me that Romanian artists and dissidents often utilized a furtive strategy for discussing the political situation through theater that was based on reinterpretations of the classics, because it was too dangerous for them to criticize their society directly. Romanian theater artists at that time filled their work with pointed clues (which they called "lizards") to guide audiences in recognizing the codes or hidden metaphors for current social affairs and to keep alive a kind of subtle resistance through a collective understanding of the madness that surrounded them. Saviana had taken an active part in this culture of alternative ideas, just as she would play an active but transformed role after 1989, since, for her, free thought ought to be a requirement under both political systems. Once, while Saviana and I were walking together through Bucharest in 2005, we passed a storefront on a narrow side street that she excitedly described as a location where she and others in a writer's group called "Universitas" had shared poetry that was directly critical of the government during the late 1980's. The censors—the political police—would monitor them closely, sometimes joining them in the dark to drink and read subversive poetry. Even then, Saviana's poems were active and theatrical, featuring characters in conflict, centering on the struggles of women. In underground venues like this one, where writers played a role in fomenting change by speaking myriad versions of the truth, Saviana the poet began to evolve into Saviana the dramatist.

In the decades after the Revolution, the Romanian theater embraced with passion and exuberance the task of leading a new and volatile society onto the world stage. But when these massive changes took place, chaos ruled at first, and so did a different kind of social and political instability. The new government struggled to manage an orderly transition to democracy and to establish a functional market economy, which was slowed by the country's lack of infrastructure, widespread corruption and the mandate to transfer property from the State to private ownership even though the legal system to support this process had not been fully formed. The public, which did not have much faith left in governmental institutions or in broad social ideologies, turned to the free market with a vengeance; many Romanians became entrepreneurs focused on accessing or distributing Western commercial products and media. The great Romanian theaters and cultural institutions, often credited with helping to bring about the Revolution, enjoyed heightened status in society, and continued to present visually stunning and complex productions—sponsored now by the newly-established democratic government and the newly-wealthy elite, instead of the Communist Party.

Saviana had worked in both underground and institutional theaters in Romania, where she had achieved significant success, as well as earned many awards (and not just as a playwright, but as a poet, too). She was among the first of her generation to recognize that the theater in post-revolutionary Romania needed to take on new challenges—to expand beyond a theater culture predominately defined by the visions of stage directors and designers in order to encompass new writing and new ideas. She had seen how, in a very short time, the theater's role had shifted from indirect criticism of political circumstances, often presented by clever directors through visual staging that was independent of the play's text, to the more complex task of rebuilding a society through the establishment of social principles in a dramatic repertoire that used language as well as visual cues to describe action. The public, which had suffered enormous and sustained trauma for decades, was mostly not yet ready to reflect on its painful history or to think very deeply about its collective responsibility to redefine its values through culture. Mainstream theaters were reluctant to support alternative voices or the ideas of its youngest artists. The social fabric of Romania was still weak, and the nation's stakeholders—even in this emerging democracy—did not encourage oppositional thinking while its institutions were stabilizing themselves.

The esteem that the British and Americans hold for playwrights was an unknown concept in Romania, where the theater culture is led by directors. (The Romanian word for "director," "regizor," is remarkably similar to "rege," the word for "king.") As a result, Saviana and some of her colleagues sought refuge in alternative venues for their more progressive writing and looked beyond Romania for new ways of expressing themselves. In the early 1990s, Britain's Royal Court Theatre was invited to lead playwriting workshops that encouraged young Romanians to write about their current circumstances. DramaFest was established as the country's first contemporary playwriting festival and, later, DramAcum, a collective, was formed by a group of directing students at the university in Bucharest to support new writing for the theater. The owner of Green Hours, a downtown Bucharest nightclub that catered to young people, invited poets and playwrights to produce their work in his smoke-filled basement bar. Saviana's play, *Infanta. Users' Guide*, written in 2000 after she had become quite well known, was staged at Ariel Theater to international acclaim by a young and controversial director named Radu Afrim, whose directing work in alternative spaces has subsequently made him into a household name in Romania and the surrounding region. A whole new generation of young artists and leaders was emerging—among them Gianina Carbunariu, Stefan Peca, and Andreea Valean—bringing alternative values to the table that challenged the old guard.

For Saviana, however, it was British playwright Caryl Churchill's arrival in Bucharest just after the Revolution that had changed the direction of her life. Churchill had come with a group of students from the

London School of Drama to create a play about Romanian society in turmoil, based on actual interviews, and the resultant play, *Mad Forest*, premiered at Romania's National Theatre in 1990. Saviana was amazed at what Churchill, partly because she was an outsider, could see about circumstances in Romania that most people inside Romania could not see. This experience inspired Saviana to begin to write plays and to travel in order to grow as an artist and activist.

Meanwhile, Saviana began to take part in new travel opportunities and programs that were being made available to Romanian artists by the government and a number of agencies including the British Council, the Soros Foundation, the Trust for Mutual Understanding, CEC Artslink, the Fulbright Program, and, later, the European Union. The catalyst that shifted Saviana's focus from poetry to playwriting came in 1998; the Du Monde Entiere, a festival at Theatre Gerard Philipe de Saint Denis in France, selected one play from each country that had qualified for the Soccer World Cup that year, and, to Saviana's surprise, the festival organizers chose her lengthy dramatic poem, *Outcast*. Romania's soccer team didn't make it to the finals, so the newspapers at home trumpeted her selection with such catchy headlines as "Romania's Boys Lose but Saviana Stanescu is Still in Competition!" Critics referred to Saviana as "the hard and brilliant poetess-playwright at the border of the millennium."

Other international commissions and fellowships followed fast. In 1999, she traveled to the Ruhr International Theatre Summer Academy in Germany on a playwriting fellowship where her teachers included David Harrower and other British and American playwrights. She received British Council fellowships to participate in the Cambridge Literature Festival in 1999 and 2000, and a Kultur Kontakt fellowship in 2000 to write a play in Vienna, Austria. With every step and every project, Saviana was building bridges that would not only serve her in her blossoming career but would pave the way for others.

In 2000, she won Romania's most prestigious prize for dramatic writing, the Best Play of the Year Award from UNITER, Romania's national union for theater artists, for *Inflatable Apocalypse*. Because Saviana was already known as a writer and critic and she did not want the judges to be influenced by those facts, and because no woman had yet won this prize, she wrote under the male pseudonym Olimpiu Dima, which was the masculine form of her grandmother's name. When the head of jury, Marian Popescu, telephoned her with the news that she had won, he was (according to Saviana) very surprised to hear a woman's voice. One of my favorite images of Saviana is encapsulated in a story about the UNITER awards ceremony that was related to me by one of her Romanian friends on my first visit to Bucharest: "Olimpiu Dima" was announced as the winner; a stunning, dark-haired woman in a shining silver dress strode confidently to the stage to accept her award; in the stunned silence, a champagne glass dropped from the hand of a surprised guest and shattered. Thunderous applause filled the hall. After "Olimpiu Dima's" victory, other women writers started to submit works under male pseudonyms.

A year later, Saviana was offered both a residency at the Royal Court Theatre in London for the months of July and August and a Fulbright fellowship to study at New York University starting in September. She had been abroad for most of the spring, working in residencies in London, Vienna and Munich. She could have continued directly to the Royal Court, but her father was suffering from terminal lung cancer, and she needed to be at home with her family before leaving for New York. She was excited about the prospect of going to America, where she hoped to learn more about how she, as a playwright, could contribute as an artist in a more democratic environment. She left for America on August 23rd,

2001, and remembers a perfect view of the Twin Towers and the New York City skyline as her plane descended into Kennedy Airport. A little more than two weeks later, 9/11 took place and everything changed again for Saviana—and for the rest of us. Visas for foreigners were canceled and U. S. immigration policies began to change quickly, along with American attitudes about the world. Saviana wasn't able to go back home to Romania for four years; she feared that she would not be able to obtain a visa to return to New York to complete her Masters degrees, first in Performance Studies and, later, in Dramatic Writing.

Saviana's rise as a New York playwright came about in tandem with her activist work on behalf of Romanian writers in the United States and, reciprocally, American writers in Romania. Recognizing that Romania's theater system has remained firmly under the control of its stage directors and managers, she has helped the Lark form and organize new programs that could foster a new playwriting culture among Romanians through travel visits and residencies in the United States. In 2005, the Lark applied for and received a New Generations Program fellowship for Saviana from Theatre Communications Group, underwritten by the Doris Duke Charitable Foundation and The Andrew W. Mellon Foundation. With this grant, we were able to hire Saviana to launch an internationally-based initiative, the American Romanian Theater Exchange program (or "ARTE") and to serve as its director while, at the same time, developing her newest play, *Lenin's Shoe*, with director Daniella Topol. Saviana has established strong relationships through ARTE with many Romanian and Eastern European artists while opening new doors for American artists—including Tanya Barfield, Catherine Coray, Gordon Edelstein, Randy Gener, Yussef El Guindi, Melissa Hardy, Rajiv Joseph, Arthur Kopit, Romulus Linney, Kelly Stuart, Lloyd Suh and Doug Wright—to see the world from a Romanian perspective through residencies there.

Saviana has also secured sustained collaborations with Dorina Lazar, the remarkable actress who heads Bucharest's Odeon Theater; Corina Suteu, the visionary director of the Romanian Cultural Institute in New York City; Alina Nelega and Gabi Cadariu, the innovative co-founders of Ariel Theater in Transylvania; Ioana Ieronim, the acclaimed Romanian poet and cultural diplomat who identified Saviana as a Fulbright scholar in 2001; and other inspiring leaders who are shaping the theater in Romania today.

Saviana's significant contributions as an artist have a great deal to do with the "bridge" metaphor. She writes often about bridge themes like migration, immigration and transformation. She commutes across a bridge connecting two languages. As a poet-turned-playwright, and in her fascination with the internet and other forms of meta-communication, she explores the bridge between ideas and action, between the surreal and the very real. As stated earlier, she is part of Romania's bridge generation: a group of outspoken artists who participated in the 1989 Revolution and began laying the groundwork for alterative arts and culture in a democratic society. Even the challenge of reframing the role of the arts in a post-revolutionary society conjures up the idea of a bridge to a future that is yet unformed. This kind of bridge is suspended between the circumstances of the present and a vision for the future. It is built from the side that is already known and stretches out to meet an unknown or perhaps nonexistent coast through the sheer force of imagination. In this way, the bridge to a new and healthy arts culture for a country like Romania, or, indeed, for any country that acknowledges the inevitability of social change, is very like the immigrant experience; no matter where in the world one travels to escape impossible circumstances, one relies on vision and imagination to transform it into a true home.

The three plays in this volume—*Waxing West, Lenin's Shoe,* and *Aliens with Extraordinary Skills*—each celebrate Saviana's love affair with New York City and are among her earliest works written in America. They explore themes of freedom, denial, displacement and survival, and they chronicle the author's evolution as a rising American playwright. Saviana's passion for New York is evident in the colorful variety and warm humanity of her characters and in the wide range of environments that they inhabit. As a dramatist, she focuses on the human experiences of her characters, their dreams of success and their struggles to survive, allowing the audience on its own to determine the political context. Whether she is exploring a couple's failure to establish intimacy in the face of mutual cultural ignorance, as in *Waxing West,* portraying a generational gap that threatens to destroy two immigrant families, as in *Lenin's Shoe,* or exposing the pragmatic outcomes of disloyalty between friends, as she does in *Aliens with*

Extraordinary Skills, she reminds us, always in very personal terms, that we are not alone in the world.

Nevertheless, her plays are also profoundly political. How could they not be? Saviana's work is rooted in her experiences as a Romanian who suffered harsh deprivations under the Ceausescu regime, joined the Revolution as a journalist and poet, struggled to help fill a cultural void after the fall of Communism, but was, ultimately, disappointed by the emergence of a new Romanian society that embraced the trappings of a Western-style market economy without creating an accompanying ethos to support it. In her writing, she cannot avoid addressing these issues. Yet her political provenance, Eastern European heritage and current immigrant status do not come close to defining the Saviana who has emerged as an American theater artist. She has become, in a few short years, an important world voice who writes in the best tradition of the Theater—seeking the universal in the specific and drawing people together from all walks of life to celebrate what they have in common.

Like most of the pioneers in America before her—immigrants by definition—Saviana has adapted quickly to her new language and culture, by diligence and necessity, and through a persistent sense of humor. I am unceasingly impressed by her remarkable mastery of the English language, an adopted language, both in conversation and dramatic writing. Saviana, who has been my friend almost from the time of her arrival in New York, has worked on at least six of her plays at the Lark Play Development Center. Even at the beginning, she was a master of the English idiom, frequently coining original phrases to great effect and applying her incredibly astute ear to capture the specific vocabulary of a teenaged computer geek, a Russian gangster, an upper-crust Ivy League graduate, or a dialect inflected by Arabic. Saviana is adept with dramatic language, and her poetry conflates sound, meaning, and action. In *Waxing West*, for example, Daniela, the Romanian cosmetologist and mail-order bride, complains wistfully in a monologue to Charlie, the American businessman and her benefactor, who, absorbed in his own thoughts, does not even appear to be listening to her. She conveys more than simply the fact that, yes, she shoplifted at the drugstore; she explains that she wants to be *seen*, to have financial freedom, to be valued, even loved; she experiences a perverse elation when Charlie loses his temper at her, though, at the same time, she doesn't want to jeopardize her comfortable situation living with him. These contradictory emotions and frustrations boil over into witty wordplay in Daniela's (and Saviana's) new language of English:

DANIELA:

It's only Vitamin C, Charlie. Orange

flavored, with rose hips. Six point eight

nine dollars… Six point eight nine

dollars are capable to drive you mad at
me, Charlie. That's how much your
"love" is worth in your opinion. Not
seven dollars, not 70, not 700... No, you
love me for exactly six dollars and 89
cents. My hips are worth less than some
chewable anonymous tablets with rose
hips.

Saviana's poetry is also tenderly evocative of
circumstance and the human condition. When Charlie
is not ignoring Daniela, playing his violin alone in his
room, or complaining to his mother (who, in an act of
beneficence, has imported Daniela from Romania to
keep her son company if and when she dies), Charlie
is capable of profound, even embarrassing, intimacy
with Daniela, playing out, for example, his sexual
fantasies of being cooked, basted and eaten like a
turkey, including gurgling "gobble, gobble" as she
carves his flesh with a plastic knife and fork. Yet,
somehow, within a landscape of awkward silences

and desperate cries for connection, this unlikely pair forms a language of their own and begins to map out a unique brand of love.

Waxing West, completed in 2003, fuses a boldly theatrical comic style, reminiscent of vaudeville and British Music Hall, with a linear story line about Daniela, a young cosmetologist from Romania who flees the squalor of her home to make her way in America. Saviana's roots in the Absurdist tradition are apparent in just about everything she writes, but, in this play, she has begun to experiment with what she sees as a particularly rational mindset that Americans bring to the theater, tempering the absurdity of Daniela's experience in her new country—our America—with a combination of comic theatricality and psychological realism. Nicolae and Elena Ceausescu appear as singing and dancing vampires, performing raucous musical numbers and telling jokes intended to crush Daniela's confidence, and thereby dash her dreams. After all, the

Ceausescus have seen their dreams collapse; why shouldn't she?

In counterpoint, Saviana presents Daniela's journey as a series of inevitable steps that take her from psychological and spiritual bondage to freedom and redemption in a new land. Daniela's act of will in exorcizing the demon imprint of her Romanian past by vanquishing the ghosts of Nicolae and Elena results in a new sense of personal freedom. What makes this play so powerful is that the act of courage that enables Daniela to achieve this freedom, and redeems her in our eyes, has made her vulnerable to pain and loss in a whole new way. For her, this is the price of freedom. When her male companion, Charlie, dies unexpectedly in the Twin Towers' collapse, she is devastated by a feeling of sadness that is new to her, that comes from within and derives from a newly held sense of accountability for her own choices and for others' pain. Perhaps she recognizes that freedom is preserved through daily acts of will and a sense of responsibility to a future which remains largely unknowable. In many ways, Daniela's experience in the play is emblematic of the journey Saviana embarked upon when she came to America as a writer in search of her American voice.

While *Waxing West* depicts an immigrant's surreal and often nightmarish path towards the American Dream, Saviana's second American play, *Lenin's Shoe*, completed in 2006, is darker and draws more specifically on Saviana's experiences as a journalist prior to the 1989 Revolution, and on her observations of Eastern European émigrés in New York City struggling to reclaim their lives and dignity. For instance, Vlad is an immigrant teenager, now living in Queens, New York, who was crippled as a child by a fragment that fell from a statue of Lenin—Lenin's shoe, naturally—as it was being pulled down by a zealous crowd of revolutionaries. Vlad is lonely, sad and isolated; he finds solace in the virtual world of blogs and in rap music which infuses his expressive

speech with its strange and often violent poetry.
Brilliant yet intensely angry, he struggles for a sense
of identity in the signs and symbols that surround
him: his paralyzing wound is a legacy of the home
and mother he barely remembers; American culture is
just outside his window, yet he is wheelchair-bound
and shielded from it by an overprotective father who
works for the Russian criminal underground; outside
on the street lives Kebab, a failed suicide bomber who
is now homeless. When Vlad's father hires the
beautiful Jasna, an unhappily married refugee and
former war correspondent, to take care of his disabled
son, the boy hatches a plan to kill his father. Though
the play finds resolution as a comedy, the pain of
displacement and traumatic stress born of violent
social unrest and war pervades this marginalized
community of immigrants, allowing the author to
explore feelings of paralysis and shame experienced
by migrants who unwillingly find themselves
strangers in a strange land, unwanted and
abandoned. Yet Saviana sees a light at the end of the

tunnel; the darkest part of the night occurs just before dawn, and, like many new Americans before her, she sees hope and freedom in the reinvention of the self in a new world.

Having traveled into the underworld and back with *Lenin's Shoe*, Saviana next turned her attention to themes of constructive engagement, social adaptability and the power of love in *Aliens with Extraordinary Skills*, an assertive and witty comedy commissioned in 2008 by The Women's Project through an Individual Artists Grant from the New York State Council on the Arts. *Aliens* focuses more on the present moment rather than the past and is more about the New York experience than about immigration. Of course, the central characters are foreigners ("aliens"), and their immigrant stories are distinctive and fundamental to their identities as newly-hatched Americans. But they have tapped into the city's heartbeat and know they are a part of it. They are ready to build a place for themselves, to dream beyond the current challenges, to negotiate the system (even U.S. Homeland Security) because they are ready—even determined—to call New York their home. Saviana breaks open the universal experience of wanting to succeed in belonging to something bigger than oneself. In this play, we recognize our "inner alien"—the part of us that is always on a journey to a place where we can more perfectly be ourselves. Ironically, this play, directed in its first production by a fellow Eastern European, Bosnian émigré Tea Alagic, hearkens back to some of the storytelling techniques that Saviana brought with her from Romania originally, including narrators that navigate the stage like Keystone Kops and clowns with big shoes and red noses. Yet *Aliens* is perhaps Saviana's most American play to date, brilliantly capturing the authentic rhythms, wit, and urgency of New York City's verbal exchanges and exploring critical American themes of individuality and conformity within a free society.

Fewer than nine years have passed since Saviana first touched down in America. When she arrived in 2001, she had already led an extraordinary life that had touched history in profound ways. Nevertheless, her time in New York has provided her with an enriched perspective that shines a light on the universal nature of her experience and her writing. She has investigated both her past in Romania and her immigrant experience in New York, and she challenges us to look at the future, along with her, through the intriguingly different lens of a changed world.

It was not until the spring of 2005 that Saviana was able to return to Romania. She and I traveled together—along with Lark artistic associate Jennifer Dorr White, who had originated the roles of Daniela in *Waxing West* and Jasna in *Lenin's Shoe*—on an exploratory trip to Bucharest to establish the Lark's American Romanian Theatre Exchange program with the Odeon Theater. Going back was not easy, Saviana discovered, because she was now invested politically, artistically and personally in two worlds. During the four years since she had left her native land, things had been changing fast—both for Romania and Saviana. A new generation of entrepreneurs had taken over the country, and the streets were full of people struggling to survive economically. It seemed to me a bit like the Wild West: life was tough, everything was possible, no holds were barred. Saviana was still famous, even after four years away. We were recognized on the streets and hailed in the newspapers and on television. But a new generation of Romanian artists had arisen in the time she had been away. Even though I have traveled to Romania with Saviana many times since then, I am moved every time I think of my first journey there and her first journey back after four years in America. I remember with profound emotion what it was like to look through Saviana's eyes at the world from which she had come and to which, she was discovering, she no longer belonged. She belongs somewhere else. I

keep hearing the words, "You can't go home again,"
ringing in my mind. She has built a bridge for herself
to another world where she is free to become the
extraordinary artist and visionary that is her destiny.
Most moving of all to me, however, is her generosity
in building bridges, through art and activism, strong
enough to carry the rest of us as we reach across the
abyss to understand a little of what Saviana already
knows.

John Clinton Eisner, Artistic Director

Lark Play Development Center

January 8, 2010

WAXING WEST

A Hairy-tale in Two Acts and Four Seasons

This play is dedicated to my father, Cornel Stanescu

Production History

Waxing West was written in 2003, during Stanescu's first year in the MFA program in Dramatic Writing at New York University, and it was produced at the Goldberg Theatre at NYU, directed by Jonathan Silverstein. Subsequently, it had a staged reading as part of the Immigrants Theatre Project's *American Dreams* Festival. In 2004, it was developed at the LARK Play Development Center in New York where it had a *barebones* production directed by Michael Johnson-Chase (original cast included: Jennifer Dorr-White, Kathryn Grody, Michael Bakkensen, Glynis Bell, Tom Ligon, Connie Nelson, Wayne Schroder). In 2005, it had readings at the New York Theatre Workshop, directed by Daniella Topol, and at Women's Project. In 2006, *Waxing West* had a staged reading in San Francisco at the Playwrights' Foundation/Traveling Jewish Theatre, directed by Amy Mueller, and in Los Angeles at Actors' Studio, directed by Cosmin Chivu. It was also produced in

Romania at the National Theatre in Cluj, directed by Marcy Arlin and Chris Nedeea. The first professional off-Broadway production of Waxing West opened in April 2007 at La MaMa Theatre in New York, directed by Benjamin Mosse, produced by East Coast Artists with the support of the Romanian Cultural Institute in New York. It received rave reviews in the *New York Times*, *Backstage*, and *nytheatre.com*. The cast included: Marnye Young as Daniela, Kathryn Kates as Marcela, Dan Shaked as Elvis, Jason Lawergren as Charlie, Elizabeth Atkeson as Gloria, Tony Naumovsky as Uros, Grant Neale as CEAUŞESCU/Dracula, and Alexis McGuinness as Elena. The Production Staff included: Adam Ganderson, Stage Manager; Kanae Heike, Scenic Design; Alixandra Gage, Costume Design; Sharath Patel, Sound Design; and Lucian Ban, Composition. The production toured Romania in the summer of 2007 being presented in Bucharest at ACT Theatre and in the official selection of Sibiu International Theatre Festival in Transylvania (Sibiu was the 2007 Cultural Capital of Europe).

Characters

The Romanians:

DANIELA: early thirties, cosmetologist

MARCELA: her mother, mid-fifties.

ELVIS: her brother, early twenties.

The Americans:

CHARLIE: late thirties, computer engineer

GLORIA: Charlie's sister, late forties, feminist visual artist

UROS: thirties, a homeless Muslim Yugoslavian who lost a leg in the war

The Ghosts:

CEAUŞESCU/DRACULA: former Romanian dictator, currently a vampire

ELENA: his wife, an insatiable vampiress

Setting

When: 2000–2001

Where: Bucharest and New York

Notes

Scene titles can be projected or written on a big screen, slide, sign, paper, or whatever. A slash in the dialogue - / - indicates that the next actor should start their line, creating overlapping speech.

ACT I

The actors are lined upstage, hidden in the semi-darkness.
They may be present onstage at all times, body-reacting to
DANIELA's actions and words. Violin music. Lights up on
DANIELA. She's wide-eyed, panting. She crosses
downstage.

DANIELA (*to the audience*): I have to calm down. To
calm down. To breathe deeply. Deeply. (*she does so*)
Yes. Okay. Here is the story. The whole story.
Nothing but the story. My story. Yes. Everything that
happened... (*breathing deeply like in a yoga exercise*) Tell
the story. The story... MY story, MY story. (*She calms
down.*)

I am Popescu Daniela, nationality: Romanian, age: 32,
height: 165 centimeters, color of eyes: black, passport
number: 2670222, sex: female, tourist visa number:
555257, EXPIRED, accent: strong, hair: long, place of
birth: Bucharest, place of death: to-be-announced...
You're not from the police, are you? Or from INS? No,
you don't look like...

Let me tell you this: I should be Daniela Aronson.
Daniela Aronson! Nationality: American. Age: 27?
Height... 175. Color of eyes: blue!... Charlie has small
round blue eyes... Blue bonbons on the snow... This is
the first thing I noticed in the photo his mom sent to
my mom: Sweet. Double sweet. But why is he so
sad?... (*memories invade her*)

ALL (*except DANIELA*): ONE! (*Violin music stops.*)

On the screen is written:

1. AN OLD LADY'S VISIT (THE VERY
BEGINNING)

April 11, 2000: Bucharest

DANIELA: Bucharest, Romania. An old lady's visit.
The very beginning...

*Bucharest, Romania. An apartment in Cringasi, a
working-class neighborhood. A modest living room that
also serves as a bedroom for ELVIS, DANIELA's brother.
A big calendar with American cars hangs on the wall.
ELVIS is watching TV. His legs are resting relaxed on a
small table. MARCELA is tidying the living room.*

MARCELA: How many times do I have to tell you to take your stinky paws off the table? How old are you now, Elvis?

ELVIS: You know better than I.

MARCELA: Elvis!

DANIELA (*to the audience*): My mother, Marcela, is an Elvis Presley fan.

MARCELA (*to ELVIS*): Dirty impudent giant! I don't know who you take after. Your father was such a clean sensitive polite perfect gentleman.

ELVIS: Sure. That's why he lost everything we had and ended up in jail.

MARCELA: He was in jail for political reasons, stupid Jumbo! Nobody had the courage to start a strike during that bloody *Ceauşescu* regime, but your father... your father... did.

She starts crying.

ELVIS: Whatever.

MARCELA: It is not "whatever," it is your father!

ELVIS: You used to call him: useless bastard, insignificant bag, rag, and... (*tapping the table*) piece of furniture.

MARCELA: I / never...

DANIELA and ELVIS: You always!

MARCELA (*wiping the table frantically*): Well, he didn't manage to make any money AFTER, did he?... All the smart guys in Romania, in Russia, in the whole Eastern Europe, did what was to be done, robbed the damn dead socialist state, seized those ugly gray factories, buildings, lands, *Ceauşescu's* gold, something, everything, everybody with a tiny bit of brain stole what was to be stolen, and everything was to be stolen, in '90, in '91, even in '92, one could make a fortune in a blink, one smart enough to be in the right place at the right time and sign a damn piece of paper, "this factory is mine," "those tons of oil are mine," "I'm the owner, I sell them to you," to the foreigners, to the Americans, for dollars, REAL money, that's all, MONEY, privatizing yourself, bribing who was to be bribed, opening businesses! Everybody moved around but your father...

ELVIS: Played chess in the park with the other retired guys.

MARCELA: "I cannot lie," "I cannot steal from the public wealth," like there was anyone there to judge him if he would. Everybody was doing the same. Everyone who had the / brain to...

ELVIS: He had lung cancer!

She starts crying again.

MARCELA: He was such a tender, well-raised, well-cultured, outstanding gentleman... I'm sure his soul eats at the dinner table with angels up there in Heaven, forgetting about us, his poor neglected / family...

ELVIS: Alright, alright. Stop crying. I take my feet off the table. Okay?! You may wipe it now. Stop crying.

She starts wiping the table frantically.

MARCELA: Aren't you going out with your buddies?

ELVIS: I feel like watching TV. It's too rainy outside.

MARCELA: You said something about going to a movie with the other guys...

ELVIS: I'm watching THIS movie on TV now.

DANIELA (*to the audience*): "Die Hard Three: Die Hard with a Vengeance."

MARCELA: I have someone coming over in half an hour.

ELVIS: You finally got a lover?

MARCELA: Elvis! I respect the memory of your father. I don't invite men home. To OUR home. I don't think of men. I mean I don't need men. I mean the way you think in your rotten pervert mind. I think of men /...

ELVIS: Whatever...

MARCELA: ...for your sister!

ELVIS: Oh no. We're waiting for a suitor. Does Dani know about this?

DANIELA: Not yet.

MARCELA: Could you be nice for a moment...

ELVIS: I'm all ears...

MARCELA: There is... this AMERICAN lady: Mrs. Aronson. Are you listening to me?

ELVIS passionately watches a TV sequence.

ELVIS: Yeah, yeah.

MARCELA: She had a Romanian cleaning lady for twenty years. She LOVES Romanians. Are you following?

ELVIS: The American grandma is coming to visit us. Why? (*looking at her*) I hope you're not trying to marry me to her.

MARCELA: You! You! It's not about you. It's about your sister, dummy. She's thirty-ONE!

ELVIS and DANIELA: So?

MARCELA: She doesn't have ANY boyfriend. Any prospects of getting married.

ELVIS: Come on. She's pretty enough.

MARCELA: Of course she's pretty. But she won't meet a man in that awful beauty salon... She's wasting her youth, poor little dear, waxing all those rich cows / who made illegal money after the revolution.

DANIELA: ...who made illegal money after the revolution...

ELVIS: Jesus! Don't start again with the making-money-after-the-revolution "CD," please.

MARCELA: Your sister has the chance to marry an American. An American BUSINESSMAN. Mrs. Aronson's son, Charlie! Rich, decent, well-educated. American! The luck-rain has come down over Daniela. She is going to go to America and take all of us there!

ELVIS: I don't wanna go to America.

MARCELA: You're stupid. But not that stupid.

ELVIS: I bet Dani doesn't like your idea either.

DANIELA: You bet.

MARCELA: God, why did you punish me with such kids? (to ELVIS) Have you heard about Mrs. Luca's sons? They made lots of money in Switzerland, working in civil engineering. When you finish the college your sister is PAYING for, you could go to Switzerland and make some good money in construction.

ELVIS: I hate engineering. I wanna be a film director.

(*He makes a frame with his hands and pretends he is shooting.*)

MARCELA: I don't want to hear that nonsense anymore. Your sister waxed the soul out of her with those fat cows to pay your taxes... I'm not listening to such nonsense. And take your paws off the table please!

The bell rings.

MARCELA: There she is! Could you go to the bedroom, honey...

ELVIS: This is my bedroom; did you forget?

MARCELA: Please, sweetie...

ELVIS: I'm watching TV.

The bell rings.

MARCELA: You may take the TV set with you, sweetie pie!

ELVIS doesn't move.

ELVIS: Tell the American grandma we need a VCR.

MARCELA: We are not beggars!

The bell rings again.

ELVIS: Just don't sell Dani for less than a VCR, a DVD player, and a video camera!

DANIELA: Jesus!

MARCELA: I am going to sell YOU for a hamburger, insensitive monster!

The TV can be heard louder and louder, machine guns and people dying, moans and roars, the usual thriller's soundtrack. DANIELA covers her ears. ELVIS zaps the remote control randomly. MARCELA shouts at him. The bell rings.

Blackout.

Lights on the TV set and on DANIELA. She takes her hands off her ears, looking like she's prepared for something bad to happen.

On the screen is written:

2. THE FIRST NIGHTMARE

TV ANCHOR: Comrade Nicolae *Ceauşescu*, the former Romanian president, who was executed on Christmas night in 1989, and Academician Doctor Engineer Comrade Elena *Ceauşescu*, his wife, are now vampires. They were separated after their death: *Ceauşescu* was in the Middle East, Elena worked and lived in New York. Despite their busy tooth-in-neck nightlife, they are quite unhappy. Both miss home and are nostalgic about going back to Romania and sucking some delicious Romanian blood, the blood of their human life, the blood of their "childhood" as VAMPIRES...

Lights on CEAUŞESCU.

TV ANCHOR: And now we take you LIVE to Bellu Cemetery in Bucharest, where *Ceauşescu* has just arrived. Elena is not here yet. A nice summer night. A tombstone. THEIR tombstone, on which angry revolutionaries wrote heart-felt obituaries such as: / "FUCK YOU, DICTATOR!", "POO, POO, WE'VE GOT RID OF YOU!", "YOU, CLOWN, IN THE CIRCUS OF HUNGER, YOU VAMPIRE!"...

ELVIS, DANIELA, and MARCELA: "FUCK YOU, DICTATOR!", "POO, POO, WE'VE GOT RID OF YOU!", "YOU, CLOWN, IN THE CIRCUS OF HUNGER, YOU VAMPIRE!"...

TV ANCHOR: The centre piece of *Ceauşescu* 's new Romania was built on the rubble of Bucharest's old quarter; twenty-six churches and over 7000 houses were destroyed to make way for the Civic Centre. Here looms the infamous PALACE OF THE PEOPLE, the third biggest building on earth after the Pentagon and the Tibetan Potala. Over 20,000 laborers and 600 architects toiled to build the Palace to *Ceauşescu* 's exacting standards...

CEAUŞESCU makes an abrupt "stop this program!"
gesture and goes to the tombstone with his name on it.

CEAUŞESCU: They put up a stone from my Palace of the People!... A stone from MY palace. Where did they take it from? From MY bathroom with the golden taps? From my living room with the golden carpets? From my study with the golden pens I never used? From MY... (*crying*) OUR bedroom with the golden sheets...

Lights on ELENA.

ELENA: That's my golden Nick!

CEAUȘESCU: Leni? I'll be shot and damned! It's really you. In blood and bones. I thought you were having fun in New York, sucking capitalist blood in a socialist, democratic way. (*beat*) You miss our old golden times too?...

ELENA: To be honest, I prefer golden showers in Times Square. I'm having much more fun now that I travel by myself and have dinner with people...

CEAUȘESCU: Don't tell me anymore about your capitalist lovers... enemies of the people... foreign spies... Americans. Germans. British. Aristocrats. Blue blood. Bleah bleah bleah! (*beat*) You didn't miss me...

ELENA: I missed our dogs. I missed Bucharest...

DANIELA (*talking to her father's tombstone*): Dad...

CEAUȘESCU: I'm not her dad, why is she calling me Dad? (*beat*) Maybe she means DEAD.

ELENA: You used to be the Father of these People.

CEAUȘESCU: Talk to her, you're the Mother!

ELENA: I'm not her mother. She's too... old!

CEAUȘESCU: Shall we drink her then?

ELENA: We need golden champagne glasses.

CEAUȘESCU (*nostalgic*): My 216 golden glasses from China, the gift from my old pal Mao... (*shouting*) Mao! Mao!

ELENA: Shhhhhh! You sound like a stupid tomcat.

CEAUȘESCU: I miss Mao... (*pointing at DANIELA*) Shall we ...

ELENA: Of course, darling. Cheers! Romanian blood again!

CEAUȘESCU: Cheers!... No! It's too easy. She said some awful things about us.

ELENA: This ungrateful worm? She must pay then. Let's suck her!

CEAUȘESCU: I have to come up with a plan... With a strategy...

ELENA: "1001 ways of torturing a stubborn enemy." I remember all of / them.

CEAUȘESCU: Your unpublished book!

ELENA: What about this one: electric shocks in her vagina!

CEAUȘESCU (*turned on*): Electric shocks!

ELENA (*turned on*): Or the cooking game!

CEAUȘESCU: When we starved that Enemy of the People for ten days, then ate sarmale in front of him!

ELENA: It's only a matter of finding her Weak-Spots...

CEAUȘESCU: Remember that imaginative torture session when that midget intellectual resisted for three days? What a man!

ELENA: Oh, yes, yes, years and years ago... (*laughing*) You were ready to give up!

CEAUȘESCU: You found his Weak-Spot-of-the-First-Degree...

ELENA: ... and got all the info you guys hadn't been able to scoop out of him in forty hours!

CEAUȘESCU: You are so... powerful!

ELENA: You are so... visionary!

They kiss, forgetting about DANIELA.

DANIELA: It was only vitamin C, Dad...

On the screen is written:

3. A STOLEN VITAMIN C JAR

March 22, 2001: New York

The living room of an Upper East Side New York apartment. A big calendar with Romanian monasteries hangs on the wall. DANIELA walks back and forth in front of CHARLIE who's working on a laptop. She has a vitamin C jar in her left hand and gesticulates with it, making funny noises.

DANIELA: It's only vitamin C, Charlie. Orange flavored, with rose hips. Six dollars and eighty-nine cents... six dollars and eighty-nine cents is capable to make you mad at me, Charlie. That's how much your "love" is worth in your opinion. Not seven dollars, not seventy, not 700... No, you love me for exactly six dollars and eighty-nine cents. My hips are worth less than some chewable anonymous tablets with rose hips...

(beat)

Okay, Charlie. It's your choice. I don't want to remind you what I do for you for FREE. I don't smoke here. I cook for you. Romanian food!... I hate Romanian food, Charlie, I hate "sarmale" and "mamaliga," and the Romanian traditional smell, and the Romanian exotic flavors, and the Romanian claustrophobic kitchens, but for you, Charlie, I stick two cotton pads in my nostrils, I play my energizing tape with applauses, and I do it for you, Charlie, I cook for you, although I hate this verb COOK and I plan to make it disappear in all languages.

(CHARLIE sighs. Lights on CEAUŞESCU and ELENA. They sigh mockingly.)

And it's not only about cooking, Charlie, although everything is about cooking. I play with you, that silly Thanksgiving game you love, every Sunday at six pm, you get all naked except for your white silly socks, and you take the "turkey" position, and I have to pretend that I put you in the oven, and that the fire goes stronger and stronger, and I have to see your silly dick reacting to that, Charlie, instead of my body, I have to act as if I cook you, Charlie, because you're a turkey, and I have to show you a plastic knife and

say, "Oh, I'm gonna eat you turkey," and I play this
silly part, Charlie, and see you coming and shouting
out of PLEASURE when I start cutting you with the
plastic knife, and I have to say "Oh, you're such a
good turkey, yum-yum," but I don't yum-yum, and I
don't like to yum-yum, and I generally don't eat meat,
so I yum-yum only for your sake...

(CHARLIE giggles. CEAUȘESCU and ELENA giggle
with him. He turns off the laptop and looks at DANIELA.)
And now you're mad at me because I STOLE this
damn plastic jar: orange flavored chewable vitamin C
500... I just took it from the shelf and put it in my bag.
The Calvin Klein bag you gave me for Christmas.
Nobody saw me, so what's your problem, Charlie?
And you know what: the bag from you is not a real
Calvin Klein!

CHARLIE pulls her down on the sofa. They start wrestling
or making love, it is not very clear. CEAUȘESCU and
ELENA applaud and mock DANIELA.

CEAUȘESCU: Oh, poor girl!

ELENA: It's not a real Calvin Klein!

CEAUŞESCU: Cook me! Cook me!

ELENA: You're a turkey, you're a turkey!

CEAUŞESCU and ELENA: Yum-yum! / Yum-yum!

DANIELA (*to the audience*): Four! Gloria's studio in Brooklyn. Very stylish. She bought the most expensive wax, transparent gloves, and even a white work robe for me... I can't take my eyes from two inflatable women wrestling or... making love in the middle of the floor. They look identical except for a small detail: one has her mouth open, the other one has it closed. I've never seen such an art work. I think it's beautiful. But I'm not an art critic. This may not be the right thought.

On the screen is written:

4. WAXING AND TALKING ABOUT WAXING AND TALKING
April 28, 2001: New York

GLORIA's studio in Brooklyn. A big calendar with art reproductions hangs on the wall. GLORIA lies on a sofa covered with a cotton sheet while DANIELA waxes her legs. A big installation called "Inflatable Gender" consisting of two inflatable women making love presides in the middle of the room.

GLORIA: I'm so glad you came over. You spend too much time alone in my brother's only-for-you cage. How long have you been in New York now, four months?

DANIELA (*applying wax to GLORIA's leg*): Three and a half.

GLORIA: And you never ever came to see me.

DANIELA: I came to wax you. (*She covers wax with a cloth-like strip, pressing firmly.*)

GLORIA: Now. Because I asked you.

DANIELA: I like working. (*She pulls off the strip.*)

GLORIA: Oh! Yes... It's a shame you can't open a beauty salon in New York.

DANIELA (*applying wax to GLORIA's leg*): I don't have a work permit... I don't have money... My tourist visa has expired...

GLORIA: Charlie should marry you as soon as possible.

DANIELA: He said he would. (*She covers wax with a cloth-like strip, pressing firmly.*)

GLORIA: When? You have to start planning. I can help organize the wedding...

DANIELA: On his vacation... (*She pulls off the strip.*)

GLORIA: Ah! In the summer then. (*beat*) Shame Mom will miss it. It was her idea after all.

DANIELA (*applying wax on GLORIA's leg*): I'm so sorry Mrs. Aronson died... She was such a vivid person.

GLORIA: Yeah, Mom was somebody.

DANIELA (*she covers wax with a cloth-like strip, pressing firmly*): He never talks about her.

GLORIA: Charlie?... He's a weird guy. (*DANIELA pulls off the strip.*) Ah!

DANIELA: Did it hurt?

GLORIA: No. Not really. You have easy hands...

DANIELA (*applying wax to GLORIA's leg*): Good...

GLORIA: What about the women in your country?

DANIELA: It's less painful here. The wax is better.

(*She covers wax with a cloth-like strip, pressing firmly.*)

GLORIA: I mean are they still in the wife-and-mother role for a whole lifetime show?

DANIELA: I'm not sure what you mean. (*She pulls off the strip.*)

GLORIA: Well. Men and women stuff...

DANIELA: Oh... All the women I know over there are crazed to find a man. When they found one, they are crazed to keep him. Then he cheats on them with their best friend... I've heard this story thousands of times. On your belly, please!

GLORIA turns over.

GLORIA: Women like to tell their stories, don't they?

DANIELA: Don't strain your muscle!

GLORIA: It must be something special about waxing...

DANIELA (*applying wax to GLORIA's leg*): It's like fighting. Against the unwanted hair that keeps reminding you it's there, inside your skin, ready to show its ugly head... (*She covers wax with a cloth-like strip, pressing firmly.*) Like fighting against death...

GLORIA: That's original...

DANIELA: See? You spread the wax in the direction of hair growth, but pull off the strip in the opposite direction... (*She pulls off the strip.*) It hurts a bit, of course. No little victory without a little pain.

GLORIA: That's... painfully true.

DANIELA (*applying wax to GLORIA's leg*): When I was in high school, the beauty salon in my neighborhood was the best place to go. Warm and cozy. From heating the wax... I could spend days and nights there... At home it was so cold and ugly, you know, the heat was supplied in rations. (*pronounced "Russians"*)

GLORIA: Rations. Not—Russians.

DANIELA: Relax the ankle! (*pronounced correctly*) Rations... (*She covers wax with a cloth-like strip, pressing firmly.*) It was this smell of... Beauty... All those women, young, old, fat, skinny, lying there, on the same bed, fighting the same fight, believing they can change, they can become beautiful just like this, snap your fingers, pull off the strip... (*She pulls off the strip.*) When they paid, you could see in their eyes the sign of victory... I was like their... hair-fairy!

GLORIA (*applying skin relief lotion to her legs, massaging them*): And here I am joining the Beauty Club... This is really funny: I just lost my virginity... Never had a waxing before...

DANIELA: I thought so...

GLORIA: So... Do you like to wax yourself?

DANIELA: I like to see the wax destroying the hair.

GLORIA: Right...

DANIELA: No hair! Shiny thighs, calves, bellies, armpits. Perfect bodies. Each one with its own particular charm and its own sad story: the hairy tale.

GLORIA (*seductively*): Women's bodies are beautiful, aren't they?

DANIELA (*beat*): Done. You're ready.

GLORIA (*examining her legs*): Nice... Ready for what?

DANIELA stands up.

DANIELA: I must go now.

GLORIA: Charlie doesn't get home till seven or eight. Why are you rushing?

DANIELA: I have to be... somewhere.

GLORIA: Okay. Go. I'm not keeping you here by force.

DANIELA: No. You're really nice. I like to talk to you and... I love this place.

GLORIA: Relax then! (*GLORIA stands up, then sits back on the sofa.*) We can have a chat over a glass of red wine. (*She covers her legs.*) We can have a nice time together. We HAVE a nice time together.

DANIELA (*preparing to leave*): I promised Charlie I'd give back the books I stole from Barnes & Noble...

GLORIA: Oh, no.

DANIELA: It's hard. It's gonna be embarrassing to tell them: Look, I took these books, but you didn't catch me, your security system is not as good as you think...

GLORIA: We have some serious problems here. Okay. Go and give back the books. Go, go! (*beat*) We'll have a drink sometime... soon.

DANIELA walks downstage.

DANIELA (*to the audience*): Five. Everybody wants to go to America. Question mark.

On the screen is written:

5. EVERYBODY WANTS TO GO TO AMERICA?
June 26, 2000: Bucharest

The Cringasi apartment. There are lots of photos and letters on the carpet. DANIELA and MARCELA are trying to sort them out. ELVIS is watching TV. His legs rest on the table. There is a VCR on the TV, ELVIS caresses it from time to time, like it is a trophy. MARCELA shows a photo to ELVIS.

ELVIS: I don't need to see the babushkas. You need to show them to the American guys.

DANIELA: Here is a good one: "Nice affectionate decent full-figured lady, mature, down-to-earth, poor but honest, wishes to meet a financially stable generous successful gentleman, marriage-minded, athletic, well-educated, well-traveled, D/D free, to share love's tender magic. Let's welcome sunrises and sunsets together!" I bet she copied this from the "Soul and Body" personals page. She always reads magazines when I wax her...

MARCELA: How many did you bring from the Salon?

DANIELA: Fifteen! And they keep coming. I shouldn't have told anybody about the prospect of going to America.

MARCELA: What prospect? It's not a prospect. It's certain!

DANIELA: Come on, Mom. Let's have him come to Romania first. I'd like to see how we get along together before...

ELVIS: She's right. You try on a new shirt but you don't "try on" your future husband?

MARCELA: Shut up, rag head! When you get a chance like this, you take it. You don't stop to... "try it on." Look. Look how many others are in line.

ELVIS: Babushkas. Nuts. Whores.

MARCELA: Look at this one. Beautiful!

(*She lifts a photo in the air, and reads from the "CV."*)

Mrs. Horea's daughter. With two college degrees: one in art history and one in accounting! Huh? (*to Daniela who doesn't react to this*) And she's twenty-eight!

(*to ELVIS*) Your sister must learn to see REALITY. Her mind "travels" in the clouds, in the sky, I have told her thousands of / times...

DANIELA: Would you stop talking as if I'm not here or I'm... retarded!

ELVIS: Tell her you don't want to go to America and marry that... Charlie Big-Dick.

MARCELA: Mind your words, selfish animal! She will have EVERYTHING. Robots that clean the house for you. Machines that cook by themselves. Money that is invisible numbers on a small card like this! (*She shows an imaginary card using her thumb and forefinger.*)

She won't have to worry about anything. She can have her mind settled in the clouds forever. Of course she wants to go to America. (*to DANIELA*) Don't you, honey?

DANIELA (*studying another photo and the letter attached*): This one doesn't want to get married. Listen: "Dear Miss Daniela, I know that at my age I don't have any chance to marry an American. And, truth to be told, I don't want to marry one of them. I've heard they are weird. They sleep with guns under their pillows. They have drugs for breakfast everyday. And put drugs in your coffee if you're not careful. But maybe you can find me a job as a cleaning lady there. For one year, no more. Just as long as I can make some money to pay for the heat in winter. After that I'll forget about your Americans and come back home, where I belong, to die in peace. Please, help me. I will pray for you every Sunday at church."

MARCELA (*crying*): This is poor Mrs. Ionescu from the third floor. She's alone.

DANIELA: We should lend her some money.

MARCELA: Ah, you loser. If you keep thinking like this, you'll be a loser even in America. This is how people get rich there: they take care of each Mr.

Green, they save every cent. There is no such thing as "lend" if you don't get something in return.

ELVIS: She can help cleaning this place.

MARCELA: Are you suggesting it isn't clean enough? After I scrub the soul out of me everyday...

ELVIS: That's the point. You wouldn't have to scrub it out of you. Some soul would be left for cheering us.

MARCELA throws her left slipper at him.

MARCELA: We don't have any money to lend. We barely have enough money to survive. But you wouldn't know that, parasite! (*beat*) And get your paws off the table, please.

DANIELA: Okay, okay. Could we have a bit of calm this evening?

The bell rings. MARCELA rushes to gather the photos and hide them in a drawer.

ELVIS: Another horny babushka... (*shouting*) We are not at home!

MARCELA hits him in the head with the other slipper. She rushes towards the door, off stage. DANIELA stretches her body and sighs. ELVIS takes his feet off the table and

shrugs. They look at each other, and shrug.

DANIELA walks downstage.

DANIELA: Six. The girl in the picture... Me!...

She freezes smiling like in a framed photo.

On the screen is written:

6. THE GIRL IN THE PICTURE

March 25, 2000: New York.

GLORIA and CHARLIE are in a Chinese restaurant.

They've finished the meal and are having some tea.

GLORIA: I can't believe you agreed with her! You

agreed to get MARRIED in this... odd!... ancient!...

patriarchal, old-fashioned, disgusting way.

CHARLIE: I was wondering what made you invite

me for dinner... More tea?

GLORIA: No. You have to tell her you don't want

that woman, Charlie. You don't need a female... pet

from a third-world country. You cannot let Mom feed

the illusions that you would / marry...

CHARLIE: She's invested a lot in this idea.

GLORIA: Exactly! She must forget it. As soon as possible.

CHARLIE: She wants to go to Romania and talk to the girl.

GLORIA: The woman. She's thirty-something! Look (*pointing at DANIELA*) I stole one of her pictures from Mom's bedroom. Can you believe that she framed three of this foreign woman's photos, including one with the woman at age three or four—riding a wooden horse!... All these pictures are now on OUR mother's nightstand! This Romanian cosmetologist, this Gypsy /...

CHARLIE (*looking at DANIELA*): She's not a Gypsy... She's pretty...

GLORIA: Are you racist or something?

CHARLIE: YOU said she was a Gypsy.

GLORIA: She might be. So what? The problem is that Mom has this obsession and your duty is to say NO to her. (*beat*) I thought you were gay anyway!

CHARLIE: You're wrong. Now you're gonna say I'm homophobic.

GLORIA: Are you?

CHARLIE: I'm "phobic."

GLORIA: Ha, ha. Smarty Charley...

CHARLIE: Upright Gloria...

GLORIA: Tell her you don't need a woman, Charlie!

CHARLIE (*enjoying GLORIA's growing disapproval*): I don't need a woman, Mom! I don't need an American self-righteous woman. A Latino over-talkative chick. A British snobbish giraffe. A French sexy inflatable doll. An Asian midget / mistress...

GLORIA: I knew you were a misogynist.

CHARLIE: Of course...

GLORIA: Is this because that violinist—your first and only girlfriend!—preferred *moi* to you?

CHARLIE: Yung Lee was not my only girlfriend.

GLORIA: Of course...

CHARLIE: If you don't want any more tea, I'd rather ask for the check.

GLORIA: I thought you liked Chinese food! Mom spoiled you with all those homemade / meals...

CHARLIE: It was fine, thanks.

GLORIA: I was very surprised that you decided to move out last year. Does Mom still call you two times a day?

CHARLIE: She knows I'm busy.

Beat. They both sip their tea.

GLORIA: Don't let her go to Romania, Charlie!

CHARLIE: She's looking forward to the trip.

GLORIA: She's gonna bring you a bride! Like in the worst type of soap opera... My own Mom...

CHARLIE: Be happy she's not bringing you a groom.

GLORIA: Don't be sarcastic, it doesn't suit you.

CHARLIE (*getting up*): Next time it's my treat.

GLORIA: You're impossible, I hope you're aware of this. That poor Romanian is gonna have a hard time here, the poor woman / is...

CHARLIE: Her name is Daniela.

He leaves. GLORIA pours herself more tea. DANIELA de-freezes and walks downstage.

DANIELA: Me... At my dad's grave. Bellu Cemetery, Bucharest. Smoking like a Hamletian vamp. Hiding in the smoke.

On the screen is written:

7. TO GO OR NOT TO GO

September 11, 2000: Bucharest

DANIELA lights candles at her father's tomb. It's a sunny

day. She has a cigarette in her hand but hasn't lit it yet.

Lights on CEAUȘESCU and ELENA wearing dark

sunglasses.

DANIELA: To go or not to go... What shall I do,

Dad?!... Dad?!... I hope you're fine up there... I'm not...

I know, I know...you wanted me to be somebody. To

feel proud of me. To have all your colleagues

respecting you because I'm so special... (*beat*) I'm not

so special, Dad... Better get used to this idea otherwise

you'll be up there in Heaven just as unhappy as you

were down here, on the Earth... (*She lights the cigarette*

with a candle.) Yes, I know... I should have gone to

college... But it was the Revolution... The University

Square... The new elections... The meetings against

corruption... Things were changing in Romania, I had

to be there, didn't I?... Didn't I?

CEAUȘESCU: No, you didn't!

ELENA: There was no revolution, you loser!

DANIELA: You remember the Shakespeare Club in high school!... I was good in Ophelia, wasn't I? ... I still have that tape with applauses you recorded at my graduation show...

(*She smokes like a Hamletian vamp.*)

To go or not to go... that is the question: "Whether 'tis nobler in the mind to suffer the slings and arrows of outrageous fortune, or to take arms against a sea of troubles, and by opposing end them?"...

"To die, to sleep... to sleep, perchance to dream"... Why don't you at least send me some nice dreams, papa?... Why don't you visit me as a ghost?... Maybe in that America... it's a bit, just a bit, a tiny little bit, like in the movies. You have a nice house, two floors, four bedrooms, two cars, one for you, one for your husband... breakfast and dinner with all the family... Three main courses. Two desserts! Everybody smiling! A coffee filter, a washing machine, a microwave... Those microwaves cook everything by themselves, don't they?

CEAUŞESCU: No American microwave!

ELENA: No capitalist house!

DANIELA: Our old house, the "Castle"... I can still hear the walls crumbling... / "Don't cry, my little princess, don't cry, I will build a new castle for you, I promise, my princess will be happy!"

CEAUŞESCU: Don't cry, my little "princess," don't cry, I will build a new castle for you, I promise, my "princess" will be happy!

DANIELA: You shouldn't have promised. It was such a bad joke.

ELENA: No joke...

DANIELA: Do you think that guy Charlie makes jokes?

ELENA: No American husband...

DANIELA: Can you find "instant happiness" in American stores?...

ELENA: No princess!

CEAUŞESCU: No "castle"!

DANIELA: You don't know, I know. Still ...

CEAUȘESCU (*seriously*): No aristocratic houses in my socialist republic!

ELENA (*seriously*): Demolish them!

CEAUȘESCU: Demolish them!

CEAUȘESCU and ELENA: Demolish!

DANIELA: No!... You shouldn't have smoked so much, papa...

She walks downstage, smoking.

DANIELA: Seven! (*confused*) No. Eight... Blind date. Well... almost blind.

On the screen is written:

8. BLIND DATE

May 5, 2001: New York

A bench in Central Park. DANIELA sits on a bench, smoking. CHARLIE comes. They both wear dark glasses.

CHARLIE: This must be the fifth bench from the West.

DANIELA: And the seventh from the East.

CHARLIE: Are you Daniela?

DANIELA: Charlie?

CHARLIE: Yes. May I take a seat?

DANIELA: Sure. (*She stubs and tosses out the cigarette.*)

They sit on the bench at a certain distance from each other.

CHARLIE: Beautiful weather, isn't it?

DANIELA: We agreed not to talk about the weather.

CHARLIE: Sure.

DANIELA: Let's talk about us, Charlie. Describe yourself.

CHARLIE: I dunno...

DANIELA: Are you tall, short, handsome, ugly, smart, dumb... no, forget the last two. Describe yourself physically first.

CHARLIE: I'm pretty tall.

DANIELA: Use adjectives, similes, metaphors. Try to be eloquent and poetic.

CHARLIE: I'm tall like a... like a... I'm sorry Daniela, I can't say how tall I am "like."

DANIELA: Okay. Are you fat, are you slim?

CHARLIE: So and so.

DANIELA: You know what: you're not helping our blind date to go smoothly...

CHARLIE: What about you?

DANIELA: You go first. Then I go.

CHARLIE (*struggling to please her*): I'm tall like an oak tree grown by the sun, I'm thin like a... barbed wire. I'm silent like a fish and blind like a jellyfish.

DANIELA (*laughing*): It doesn't work!

CHARLIE gets closer to her and starts caressing tenderly her shoulders.

DANIELA: What are you doing? This is a public space. People can see us.

CHARLIE (*trying to hold her in his arms*): We cannot see them.

DANIELA (*jerking away*): What do you think of me? I'm not the sort of woman who lets herself be touched all over at the first blind date.

CHARLIE (*with faked pathos*): My eyes are in my fingertips. Touching means seeing for us.

DANIELA: You're not able to say anything really nice. You turn me off.

CHARLIE (*taking distance again*): You turn me off too.

DANIELA: Good.

CHARLIE: Great.

DANIELA: Excellent.

CHARLIE: YOU had this silly idea...

DANIELA (*taking off her glasses*): I thought that playing blind would help, but you're a catastrophe at it.

CHARLIE (*taking off his glasses*): I thought we wouldn't talk so much if we played blind.

DANIELA: I thought we'd have fun if I could extract you from your Siamese laptop. For a different kind of game. Nothing about turkeys, everything about us! (*Pause. CHARLIE plays with his cane.*) To go out, to play a little in the fresh air, to smell the spring, maybe to have a nice dinner and talk about us...

CHARLIE: I took you out for tea and cookies last Sunday.

DANIELA: Yes. At the Blood Donors Center. Tea and cookies for free.

CHARLIE: There's nothing wrong with giving blood. You can help people in need.

DANIELA: Sure.

CHARLIE: You gave all my old shirts and trousers to that dirty homeless guy in the Times Square subway.

DANIELA: Uros.

CHARLIE: This morning I couldn't find my silver watch (*beat*)... the one that goes with the grey suit. (*beat*) And I had a meeting with a client.

DANIELA: You still have three wrist watches. (*beat*) I took the ugliest one.

CHARLIE: You stole it.

DANIELA: I gave it to Uros.

CHARLIE: I don't want to hear about that crippled Muslim bum anymore.

DANIELA: He used to teach philosophy and dead languages before the war. In Yugoslavia.

CHARLIE: That ragged guy in the wheelchair?!

DANIELA: His dream is to follow Gilgamesh's traces.

CHARLIE: Whose traces?

DANIELA: Gilgamesh. You don't know the story? Looking for eternal life, his friend Enkidu...

CHARLIE: We should go home. It's late.

DANIELA: He wants to go to Iraq, Iran, Syria... in Gilgamesh's footsteps!

CHARLIE: He's crazy. And he's got my watch for that?

DANIELA: He has a fire inside him...

CHARLIE: What about my fire...

He starts kissing her. She pushes against him for a while, resigns for a moment, then pushes him away angrily.

DANIELA : Nine! (*to the audience*) You must meet Uros! About life and death in Times Square...

On the screen is written:

9. ABOUT LIFE AND DEATH IN TIMES SQUARE
May 15, 2001: New York

Times Square subway station. DANIELA pushes UROS's wheelchair in an area with a NO ENTRANCE sign.

UROS: I and the rats. Sharing the "luxurious apartment" they offered me.

DANIELA: You're very lucky they allowed you to live there, Uros!... I can get a TV set for you, / I...

UROS: That's nonsense... What am I supposed to do with a TV set? Where would I plug it? *(laughing and coughing)* In my homeless buddies' asses? *(beat)* No, gimme a radio. Can you bring me a radio from your millionaire man?

DANIELA: Charlie is not a millionaire. *(beat)* You are already wearing his shirt and his trousers. His dark red socks. His silver watch. His tie.

UROS: I don't need his tie! *(He pulls it off.)* Can he spare some money for a plane ticket? A one-way ticket. Let's not ask too much.

DANIELA: You must SEE the news. It's not safe there. You cannot go there. Not in your condition.

UROS: Listen, girl: Uros goes wherever he wants to go. He's not a chicken, he's a man. *(laughing and coughing)* And now that he has two wheels and one leg, he's more than a man. He's a willing chair...

DANIELA: Wheeling! ... I'm telling you, Iraq, Iran, and Syria are not safe now. Of course you can go, but it's not smart to go. It's dangerous!

UROS: It was dangerous in Gilgamesh's time. It's dangerous today. It will be dangerous tomorrow. I don't need to watch the news to find out such a simple truth... Come, sit on my "armchair"!

DANIELA (*sitting on the wheelchair's right arm*): Your obsession with Gilgamesh's story... What's so special? A guy and his friend...

UROS: A king and his friend Enkidu...

DANIELA: ...traveling in search of...

UROS: Immortality! (*He slaps her thigh.*)

DANIELA: You cannot believe in immortality!

UROS: Of course, not... Mrs. Death and I are old pals. She follows me like a shadow. She clings to me like a spider. She's the tie around my neck... I want to take her with me on Gilgamesh's traces. To see her grimace there, on the land where she was defeated.

DANIELA: She was never defeated, Uros.

UROS: Yes, she was. (*He puts his hand on DANIELA's leg.*)

DANIELA: You saw her in your war. In Yugoslavia.

UROS: Of course I saw her. She gulped my left leg. Gulped my wife Jasna. Gulped my son Andrej. Gulped my daughter Tanja. But she spewed me out. I was too much for her bowels. That's why I want to take her on a "honeymoon." To Iraq.

DANIELA: Do you want to go to... fight there?

UROS: You may say so. (*He strokes DANIELA's thigh.*)

DANIELA: Do you want to die there? (*She jerks away.*)

UROS: I just want to go there. (*pause*) Could you push me back to my stinky dark solitary corner? Home bitter home...

DANIELA pushes his wheelchair back.

UROS: Did you steal that book from Barnes & Noble? Gilgamesh's epic?

DANIELA: I did.

UROS: Did you use the strategy I taught you?

DANIELA: Yes. Pay for one book, put three or four in your bag.

UROS (*laughing*): They never check your bag if you pay for one. Sit here (*patting with his palm the arm of the wheelchair*) on my armchair! (*she sits*) Did you have a good time stealing?

DANIELA: It was... exciting. To steal books is not something bad, is it?

UROS: No, girl. It's love of literature. It's not stealing. It's passion for culture. For knowledge... It's to choose to live a spiritual life over a material one. They can stick their money up their asses! Books are what matter. Stories. There's no price for that. (*He touches her again, more passionately.*) You cannot trade everything. There are some things above shopping. You understand that, you're a smart / girl...

DANIELA: What are you doing?

UROS: Life cannot be only shopping and fucking.

DANIELA: I gave back the books. (*She tries to get away, he holds her.*)

Lights on CEAUȘESCU and ELENA looking amused.

UROS: You didn't read the Gilgamesh?

DANIELA: No! (*She jerks away.*) Don't do that again, Uros! You're my friend. My only friend. / Don't...

UROS: Relax, girl. Uros is your friend!

DANIELA walks downstage.

ELENA: Her friend.

CEAUŞESCU: An old comrade from Yugoslavia. Tito's guy.

ELENA: Her FRIEND!

CEAUŞESCU: Yes.

ELENA: Friend! Supporter. Mate. Well-wisher.

CEAUŞESCU: Exactly.

ELENA: Someone she cares about.

CEAUŞESCU: Yes. So?

ELENA: Weak Spot—of the Second Degree!

CEAUŞESCU: Oh. I got it!

ELENA: You used to be much much much faster.

CEAUŞESCU: What shall we do then? How shall we do?

ELENA: A trial first.

CEAUŞESCU: No, not a trial!

ELENA: Then an execution.

On the screen is written:

10. SECOND NIGHTMARE

DANIELA: These nightmares have nothing to do with my "real" life. They are just dreams.

ELENA: Shut up, girl!

CEAUŞESCU: Nobody gave you permission to talk.

ELENA: She's so boring, isn't she?... (*to DANIELA*) Stand up, accused!

DANIELA: I'm not guilty!

ELENA: Bitch! ... She's too talkative. She must be impaled without delay.

DANIELA: Shoot me! Please...

CEAUŞESCU: She wants to be shot...

ELENA: She's too demanding...

CEAUŞESCU: We don't like to be reminded about shootings...

ELENA: We were shot in such an unforgivable... rude aggressive provincial way. How could she mention that? She must be impaled!

CEAUŞESCU: What is this girl accused of? Theft from the socialist public wealth?

DANIELA: I haven't done anything wrong. I was sleeping in my bed.

ELENA: Naked... (*She gets up and rips off DANIELA's pajamas with a sharp motion.*) Your nipples are too small.

DANIELA: It's not my fault!

CEAUȘESCU: I don't know... I like small nipples.

ELENA: I know! She must be impaled. In her vagina.

CEAUȘESCU: That's not impaling, it's rape.

ELENA: Whatever. Let's have her impaled and put an end to this. I hate trials. They depress me.

CEAUȘESCU: They depress me too. Look, I'm so pale!

ELENA: She persists in reminding us of the worst part of our mortal life...

CEAUȘESCU: That's not nice, girl. Our trial / was nothing but a parody plotted by the foreign agencies and carried out by my own people. Poor stupid bastards, they got drunk on power. The power that I gave them! I made them. I created them. And how did they pay me back? They let themselves being manipulated by my enemies, by the Western spies, by those jackals plotting to steal our country, to destroy the Golden Dream of Communism, to steal our wealth, to steal our lives... (*He looks like he's about to have a heart attack.*) Did you work for them, girl? Confess! Who sent you here? Are you a thief? Are you a spy? (*He's in pain, he tries to calm down.*)

ELENA (*overlapping CEAUȘESCU's speech*): Ours was not a trial. They killed us with no trial. A bunch of worms. No spines, no brains. We should have kept them in the darkness forever. Send them all to prison. Starve them to death. Crash all those ugly dirty pipsqueak thieves, those Romanians...

DANIELA: Listen to me: I didn't steal from the socialist public wealth! I didn't steal!

ELENA: Socialist. Communist. Capitalist. Who cares now!

CEAUȘESCU (*to ELENA*): Let's go, sweetheart. We'll miss the book burning of my complete works.

ELENA: I'd like to see her impaled...

CEAUȘESCU: Come on, honey blood... You've seen enough impalements... I'm fed up with being a judge. I want to feel like a writer!

ELENA: You are as bad as a writer as you are as a judge. As an impaler. As a leader. As a dictator. As a vampire. As a husband...

CEAUȘESCU: I was a faithful husband!

ELENA: Exactly. (*to DANIELA*) Bye-bye, flesh pie! Write to me about the impalement!

CEAUȘESCU: Bye-bye, accused! Take care. Don't forget to write!

ELENA: In details! Everything you feel while being impaled. (*sensuously*) Everything that's going on in your bottom and in your head, small-nippled pipsqueak!

CEAUȘESCU: Use adjectives, similes, metaphors. Try to be eloquent and poetic!

ELENA: Die-die! Don't forget to wriiiiiiiite!

CEAUȘESCU: *Bye-bye!*

ELENA: Die-die!

They nod at each other and start dancing and singing in a vaudeville style.

CEAUȘESCU:

I AM A GOOD DICTATOR

EVERYONE CAN CONFESS

THE TENDER FINE IMPALEMENTS

RELIEVE YOU FROM THE STRESS

ELENA:

REPORT FOR US DEAR COMRADES

DESCRIBE YOUR DYING SEASONS

WE NEED TO KNOW EXACTLY

FOR SCIENTIFIC REASONS

CEAUŞESCU and ELENA:

BYE-BYE, DIE-DIE, COMRADE!

BYE-BYE, DIE-DIE, FRIEND!

THE BOTTOM OF THE STORY

IS ITS PERFECT END.

THE STORY OF THE BOTTOM

IS ITS PERFECT END.

DANIELA: I need a break...

Lights fade. **END ACT I**

ACT II

Lights on DANIELA, sitting on the floor with lots of books around her.

DANIELA: I've been trying. You can't say I haven't tried. I've got all these self-help books. I've written down the main ideas. (*looking down to her notes*) "Choose your Tomorrow: BEFORE—perfectionist, misunderstood, love junkie, over-reactive, self-effacing. AFTER—flexible, good communicator, self-accepting, in control, assertive."

I read them all: "I'm Dysfunctional, You're Dysfunctional," "It's Not as Bad as It Seems," "Master Your Panic and Take Back Your Life," "Twenty-One Ways to Stop Worrying," "How to Control Your Anxiety Before It Controls You," "How to Make Yourself Happy," "How To Stop Destroying Your Relationships," "Why Men Marry BITCHES," "Men Are From Earth, Women Are From Earth," "What to Do When He Has a Headache," "The Six-Second

Shrink," "Fun as Psychotherapy," "Let's Get Rational Game," "Three-Minute Therapy: Change Your Thinking, Change Your Life," "Dating, Mating, and Relating," "Unconditionally Accepting Yourself and Others," "Resolving Your Past"... Read them all... (*nervously*) But I'm afraid I'm still in the BEFORE stage. I still have emotions, feelings, confusion, anger... Those AFTER people! They must be so happy. So peaceful. So empty... Okay! Breathe deeply! Start counting to ten. Prepare yourself to relieve your anxiety. To relax. To talk. Okay. Here we go... Dammit, this is gonna be difficult! You don't have the references to our complicated Romanian Dacian Tracian Roman Ottoman Byzantine Balkan communist post-communist anti-communist pro-American history, all you know about us is Dracula-the-vampire, Ceauşescu-the-dictator, and Nadia Comaneci–the-gymnast! Anyway, Nadia is cool, she never comes into my dreams with her perfectly fit body, so forget about her, she's not in this story. I have more important, heavier, issues on my mind!

Stuff like life and death. No time to worry about my cellulite. Unless a bullet stops by IN it...

ALL: One!

DANIELA: About life and death in University Square.

On the screen is written:

1. ABOUT LIFE AND DEATH IN UNIVERSITY SQUARE

December 1, 2000: Bucharest

ELVIS and DANIELA are leaning against a wall of Bucharest University. Noises of a crowd cheering and hailing can be heard.

ELVIS: Those bastards! Extremist bastards!

DANIELA: Shhhhh! You've already got a leg hurt. Why ask for more?

ELVIS: Did you see that? The bastard kicked me with his boot. Three times!

DANIELA: If you cannot keep your mouth closed... Why tell them they are a bunch of "paranoid extremists"?

ELVIS: Nobody asked you to come with me...

DANIELA (*lighting a cigarette*): If you want to play the filmmaker role, that's fine... But a professional shoots the facts and keeps quiet.

ELVIS: Sure, a bowed head cannot be cut by the sword... (*grabs DANIELA's cigarette*) Gimme a smoke, I have to go back to work. This is gonna be a super film, have you seen those faces? A bunch of brainwashed stray dogs/...

DANIELA: I'm only saying, you should stop and THINK for a second before going back and sticking your camera in their faces... Nobody commissioned you for this film. Nobody will pay you for it. You're working for nobody. You can be killed for nothing. / I think...

ELVIS: I work for myself! What the fuck...

DANIELA (*mocking him*): I work, I don't think! (*seriously*) "We work, we don't think!" —remember the miners storming into THIS square ten years ago? Shouting and singing in the rhythm of hitting us, the anti-Iliescu protesters. What a joke. That communist "with a human-face" elected after the revolution. "We work, we don't think! We work, we don't think!"...

They took me for a student. Me and others. Who wore jeans and looked like they had a functioning / brain...

ELVIS: Geez, Dani, you look really ugly when you start talking seriously about the... (*mocking her*) "ghosts of the past"/

DANIELA: You saw them only on TV! You were a ten-year-old snotty brat. I was HERE. In '89, in '90, in '92, in 96! Here for all the protests of the opposition. Here at the revolution. Here! I've seen blood in this square! (*She grabs the cigarette from him.*)

ELVIS: Your Opposition hasn't done shit. A bunch of corrupted snobs! Your Inthhhellectuals... They got us here, in this shitty situation, and washed their hands of us. We are doing goooood! In the year of our Lord, 2000, we have to choose between the good old communist Iliescu and the bad old crazy Vadim, who declared he'd close the borders and take us back to the dark caves, (*massaging his injured leg*) where it seems we belong anyway... (*grabs the cigarette back*) Funny, isn't it? You have no choice but to vote for

Iliescu, who sent the miners to beat your ass in '90... I hope you're not going to vote for Vadim!

DANIELA: I'm not gonna vote for any one. I've had enough of all of them. I've had enough! (*beat*) I'll be in America before the elections...

ELVIS (*passing the cigarette*): Are you sure you wanna... marry that...

DANIELA: Mrs. Aronson is a very nice lady.

ELVIS: You're not gonna fuck her.

DANIELA: Hey! Mind your own ass! (*passing the cigarette*) Charlie sent you that video camera and the VCR...

People are booing in the square. Voices arguing, people running can be heard.

ELVIS (*excited*): Things are gonna take fire here. Vadim is playing dirty... Why don't you go home? (*passing the cigarette*) Go. Take care of Mom, make sure she's not asking for her heart attack...

DANIELA (*passing the cigarette*): Nothing big will happen. No fire, no fireworks. People are tired of revolutions. Don't you start a scandal, you're the only one who'll get kicked!

ELVIS (*he finishes smoking DANIELA's cigarette and tosses the butt away*): Gimme a break, you sound like a fucking old maid...

He leaves. DANIELA leans against the wall with her eyes closed. The crowd shouts and sings: "Awaken Thee, Romanian!" (the Romanian national anthem after 1989). As the noises fade off, DANIELA opens her eyes.

DANIELA (*to the audience*): Two. Sic transit gloria mundi.

Lights on GLORIA.

GLORIA: How the world's glory has passed...

DANIELA: I was good at Latin!

On the screen is written:

2. SIC TRANSIT GLORIA MUNDI
June 13, 2001: New York

GLORIA and DANIELA are in a fancy French restaurant in New York. They drink red wine.

GLORIA: To talk about Charlie? That's really why you invited me here?

DANIELA: *Yes.*

GLORIA: I thought it was a way of saying... a pretext!

DANIELA: It was the truth.

GLORIA: What's there to talk about? A man like any other man. Self-sufficient. Self-indulgent. Unreliable. Nice.

DANIELA: I don't think I understand him.

GLORIA: What's to understand?

DANIELA: I don't know. What does he want... What does he believe in...

GLORIA: Charlie believes that God is a sort of multidimensional computer scientist who designed this virtual 3-D game called WORLD or HUMANS. We are all characters in the bloody script of this bloody game. A bunch of so-called "angels" are playing with us. For better or for worse. Depending on their mood and some other factors. Anyway it's a brilliantly conceived system that functions due to the

Good-Evil dynamics. We have no control over it. We are manipulated... Something like that...

DANIELA: Sounds very... sad! Has he told you all that?

GLORIA: No. I invented everything!... Of course, he told me that. How could I come up with such a crazy thing?

DANIELA: He never talks such things with me... Mrs. Aronson /...

GLORIA: Look. Charlie and Mom didn't get along too well. She'd let him do everything, except what he really wanted: to play the violin.

DANIELA: Violin?

GLORIA: He didn't have any talent! Mom was right. So he played against her will in any way he could.

DANIELA: He won't marry me then...

GLORIA: C'mon... forget this conventional stuff with marriage and all the bullshit around it. A woman has to be her own person. To make decisions for herself. Not to cook for some self-righteous prick who thinks he does her a big favor each time he penetrates her. Be a smart girl...

DANIELA: I don't know... I guess I'm pretty conventional but...

GLORIA: But but but!... But! Not that I mind that... Say conventional again!

DANIELA (*with her exotic accent*): Conventional.

GLORIA: Even a word like "conventional" sounds sexy coming out of your mouth... (*beat*)

DANIELA: Let's go to your place, Gloria...

GLORIA: Why? You don't like it here? Is it too noisy? Too crowded? You need to smoke? Oh, sweet addictions...

DANIELA: You don't want to be with me?... I thought... I mean...

GLORIA: Oh. You want to... dot dot dot.

DANIELA: Yes.

GLORIA: Are you sure?

DANIELA: Well...

GLORIA: Are you sure? (*beat*)

DANIELA: No.

GLORIA: Listen, girl. Don't do anything you have doubts about. No matter if it's big or small. No matter who has asked. No matter whom you'll make happy. (*She raises her glass of wine.*) Shall we go then?

DANIELA sips her wine and sighs. GLORIA sips her wine and sighs. They look at each other like two old friends.

DANIELA: Shall we?

GLORIA bursts into laughter. She imitates DANIELA.

GLORIA: Shall we? Shall we? (*like a prude*) Shall we? Shaaaaall weeeeeee? (*beat, seriously*) No. Not until you are absolutely sure. Cheers!

DANIELA: *Cheers!*

Lights on CEAUȘESCU and ELENA. They have glasses in their hands. They smile and mock DANIELA.

CEAUȘESCU and ELENA: Shall we? Shall we? Cheers! Cheers! Shall we? Cheers!...

DANIELA (*to the audience*): Three. The Turkey game.

On the screen is written:

3. THE TURKEY GAME
July 12, 2001: New York

CHARLIE's apartment. Sunday evening. He is in the turkey position behind an "oven" built of a pile of shoeboxes or behind a transparent curtain. His head and his feet in white socks can be seen by the audience.

DANIELA has a knife in her right hand, pointing with it at CHARLIE.

DANIELA: I'm gonna eat you, turkey! Yum-yum... good turkey... fat turkey... Yum-yum...

CHARLIE: Gobble... Gobble gobble gobble...

DANIELA: Yes, turkey, I'm gonna jab you, turkey... thrust you... eat your meat, turkey... Yummy-yummy...

CHARLIE: Gobble gobble....

DANIELA: Good turkey...

CHARLIE: Gobble gobble, Gobble gobble ...

DANIELA: I'm gonna cut off your waddle... Yum-yum...

CHARLIE: Oh, gobble!

DANIELA: Your wings... your thighs... your breast... Yum-yum...

CHARLIE: Gobble... Cook me, mommy!

DANIELA: I'm gonna suck your bones... Yum!

CHARLIE (*climax*): Yeah!

DANIELA looks at the knife. CHARLIE closes his eyes.
Beat.

DANIELA swoops upon CHARLIE with the knife in her
hand.

Lights on CEAUŞESCU and ELENA.

DANIELA: I'm gonna prick you, turkey. Stab you.
Kill you. Murder you. Yum-yum! Bye-bye, turkey.
Die-die. Die-die!

CHARLIE: Ah!

She throws away the knife. There's blood on it. DANIELA
lies silently on CHARLIE's body. She starts crying.
CHARLIE wipes her eyes with his right hand.

CEAUŞESCU: Wow. That was good! The girl is tough.

ELENA: I was waiting for her to really cut off his
"waddle." Some true action.

CEAUŞESCU: She seemed quite active to me. She
reminds me of you!

ELENA: Oh, noooo! Take back your words
immediately! She's a silly squeamish mouse. She's

gonna apologize to him. Kiss his ass. Suck him up. I would never do such a thing!

CEAUȘESCU: That would make him a Weak-Spot-of-the-First-Degree, wouldn't it?

ELENA: Not yet. Not yet. Something is missing...

On the screen is written:

3. THE TURKEY GAME?

Lights up. Later, on the same Sunday evening.

The shoebox "oven" is still in the center of the living room.

CHARLIE's left arm is bandaged up. He is working on his laptop using only his right hand. DANIELA stands still, starring through the window.

DANIELA: Charlie... (*beat*) Charlie... (*beat*) I'm sorry... I'm so sorry... / I'm...

CHARLIE: Let's not talk about this.

DANIELA: Let's TALK about this! I'll go insane if I don't talk.

CHARLIE doesn't look at her.

DANIELA: Charlie!

CHARLIE: What.

DANIELA: I'm thinking of going back.

CHARLIE: Back?

DANIELA: To Romania. Back home.

CHARLIE (*looks at her*): Your home is here.

DANIELA: We're not married, Charlie.

CHARLIE: We will be.

DANIELA: When?

CHARLIE: In the summer.

DANIELA: It is summer.

CHARLIE: On my vacation.

DANIELA: When?

CHARLIE: When I take my vacation.

DANIELA: IF you'll take your vacation...

CHARLIE: A wedding is expensive.

DANIELA: Charlie...

CHARLIE: I have to make money for it, don't I?

DANIELA: You never talk about your mother.

CHARLIE: My mother?!

DANIELA: She asked me to marry you.

CHARLIE (*looking at her*): I know.

DANIELA: You didn't want...

CHARLIE: I didn't mind...

DANIELA (*touching his injured arm*): I'm sorry, Charlie. I'm so sorry...

CHARLIE: Relax. (*beat*) We won't play it again.

DANIELA: The Thanksgiving / game...

CHARLIE: Turkey game is over.

DANIELA: No game next Sunday?

CHARLIE: Nothing about turkeys.

DANIELA: Everything about us?!

CHARLIE (*smiling*): Maybe a turkey, for dinner, on Thanksgiving day...

DANIELA: Like everybody else.

CHARLIE: Like you and me.

DANIELA: We can invite Gloria and maybe / even ...

CHARLIE (*back to his laptop*): I hope that you're not actually seeing that homeless scum anymore.

DANIELA: Uros?

CHARLIE: Last Friday he tried to sell me my own old tie. The one with the purple hearts...

DANIELA: You didn't buy it, did you?

CHARLIE: Nope.

DANIELA: Good. (*beat*) Are you... hungry?

CHARLIE: But I gave him some money.

DANIELA: Shall I... cook something?

CHARLIE: It was my very first tie...

DANIELA: I should go back, Charlie!

CHARLIE: I was thirteen when Mom bought it for me...

DANIELA: I do horrible things here. I'm a thief...

CHARLIE: Don't worry about that tie...

DANIELA: I'm a criminal...

CHARLIE: It was a silly tie...

DANIELA: I'm no good here...

CHARLIE: You're a good cook.

DANIELA: I've never been a good cook, Charlie.

CHARLIE: What about mamaliga with cheese and sour cream?

DANIELA stares through the window. CHARLIE works on his laptop. It looks like the perfect family evening.

DANIELA walks downstage and addresses the audience.

DANIELA: Right. Something is missing... I can read in your eyes questions like: why don't you change something? Go out! Get a job as a waitress or as a... waitress, like so many illegal immigrants do. There are thousands of possibilities. You are in the city of all possibilities. Leave the jerk. Leave Charlie! (*beat*) I don't want to be a waitress. I'm a cosmetologist. I have my own... And don't call Charlie a jerk! Okay? (*beat*) Four! About death and life in Times Square.

She takes a radio from CHARLIE's living room and takes it into the new scene.

4. ABOUT DEATH AND LIFE IN TIMES SQUARE

July 29, 2001: New York

Times Square subway. UROS lies on four seats, covered by a ragged blanket. Someone plays saxophone nearby.

DANIELA stands by UROS's side, she has a small radio in her right hand.

DANIELA: Hey, Uros... Wake up! I've got you the radio!

UROS (*coughing*): What are you doing here? Traveling by subway... Bleah. Your millionaire man should send you shopping in a Mercedes... or a limo!... have you seen those huge white limos, those white earthworms, crawling out of Enkidu's nostrils (*coughing*)...

DANIELA: You're sick...

UROS: Uros is never sick, girl! You didn't read the story, you don't know shit about Gilgamesh and his friend's—Enkidu's!—death... When he, Gilgamesh, the immortal, well, almost immortal, realized that Mrs. Death was fucking around, and his best friend, his brother Enkidu—the mortal! —would cheat on him with that dirty bitch (*coughing*)...

DANIELA: I should bring you some antibiotics, not only vitamin C... But, you know, they don't sell antibiotics if you don't have a medical prescription, and you can't have one if you don't go to a physician, and you can't go to a physician if you don't have health insurance...

UROS: Relax, girl. I'm not sick. I don't need no insurance. I'm sure enough of all the shit around me. I don't need them to "insure' me (*coughing*)...

DANIELA: What about me, Uros? What if I get sick?

UROS: You can't get sick. You're a warrior, a woman warrior...

DANIELA: I hate wars! I hate to fight...

UROS: Then you're a corpse. And all these biped eagles regale themselves every day, raping you, tearing you apart (*coughing*)...

DANIELA: You're not yourself, Uros...

UROS: Wrong. I've never been more myself than now, when every inch of my flesh reminds me what a blessing and a torture this life is, biting your soul, licking it, biting it, licking it... (*He closes his eyes.*)

DANIELA: Open your eyes! Talk to me!

UROS (*his eyes closed*): I ran out of stories.

DANIELA (*taking his hand and putting it on her hip*): What about this one?

UROS (*stroking her hip gently*): Your millionaire man should buy you a white limo, should take you on a honeymoon to a bright sunny island, all this romantic shit, music... what's this music?... a saxophone... that's nice... very sensuous... very tender... I ran out of tenderness. I must be dead.

DANIELA: No! You'll go to Iraq, like Gilgamesh, you'll... start a new life there. Find that... whatever you are looking for!

UROS: Immortality?

DANIELA: Anything. Something to look forward to. To make you get up in the morning, get off the bed, start / the day...

UROS: Uros don't have no bed, girl. (*beat*) You grew to talk like them. All the American propaganda bullshit. (*beat*) Relax. I won't ask you to steal your Charlie's bed... (*coughing, opening his eyes*)...

DANIELA: There must be something I can do for you...

UROS (*clinging to her*): Don't let them steal your stories, don't let them steal your thoughts...

DANIELA: Who are THEY, Uros?

UROS (*he closes his eyes again*): The worms. The earthworms in the white limos. They have the power. The money. They trade your limbs, your organs, your life, your time. Even your stories! But they cannot trade your thoughts (*laughing and coughing*), even THEY cannot...

DANIELA: Where are they?

Lights on CEAUŞESCU staring at UROS.

UROS: Everywhere. They follow you. They stick on you like leeches. You cannot get off this marsh...

DANIELA: Shhhhhhhhh. You must rest now...

UROS: I thought you were smart, girl... I thought you were... you... you... you (*He falls asleep.*)

CEAUŞESCU (*to UROS*): Immortality is for people of vision and power, old comrade. Have you led any country? Have you created any policy? Have you improved the human race? Have you built a palace? Have you had breakfast with the Queen of England or George Bush? Have you had dinner with Saddam Hussein or Yasser Arafat? Have you had millions of people worshiping your name? Have you had your portrait in all classrooms? Have you been on the first page of every book in your language? Have you sentenced anybody to death? Have you sentenced anybody to life?... Have you been betrayed and killed by your own people?

DANIELA: Don't listen to him, Uros! Don't listen to him! (*to the audience*) Five! Goodbye, Romania. (*beat*) An end.

On the screen is written:

5. GOODBYE, ROMANIA! (AN END)

January 13, 2001: Bucharest

Otopeni Airport. DANIELA and MARCELA, sitting next to each other. Noises of planes taking off. Noises of people jostling around. MARCELA is crying.

DANIELA: C'mon, Mom... There are people looking at us.

MARCELA: Only one daughter and she is going to be thousands of kilometers away... across the ocean... and the whole of Europe...

DANIELA: You wanted me to marry an American. Be happy. I'm gonna marry one.

MARCELA: Take care not to make a shame of my name there, in America!

DANIELA: Sure. Everybody knows you over there.

MARCELA: Behave right! Don't swear. Don't smoke... Don't eat with your elbows on the table... Don't chomp... Don't drink water during the main dish... (*beat*) Wash your underwear every night before you go to bed. Change it for a new one in the morning. I put twenty pairs of panties in your small baggage...We don't want your husband to think we're dirty!

DANIELA: My future husband. (*beat*) I hope he's a nice guy.

MARCELA: He's a BUSINESSMAN!

DANIELA: He's not a businessman, he's a computer engineer. He works at the sixty-sixth floor of this sky / scraper...

MARCELA: You are so lucky! You won't have to cook and scrub like me everyday, no vacation, no weekend, no fun / for fifty years...

DANIELA: for fifty years... I know, I know. I'm not gonna cook, I'm not gonna scrub. I can promise that.

(*raising her voice*) Mrs. Aronson / has a cleaning lady anyway.

MARCELA: She's your husband's mother! You shouldn't raise your voice at her as you do with me! Watch your behavior! You are going to live with her before the wedding, she will test you... (*looking around*) Where is that Elvis? He will miss saying good bye to his own sister.

DANIELA: We still have more than two hours. You insisted we were here three hours in advance.

MARCELA: You never know with airports. Better waiting than crying because we missed the plane... (*beat*) Don't forget: you have five suitcases. The big brown one the with clothes, the small green one with the presents, the dark blue bag with your wedding dress... (*starts crying*) I am not going to be at my own girl's wedding...

DANIELA: I told you it'd be better to ask HIM to come here...

MARCELA: That's silly. What if he didn't like you...

DANIELA: If he doesn't like me...

MARCELA: Nonsense. He is going to love you if you behave right... Where is that Elvis?... So... you have five suitcases: the brown one, the small green one, the dark blue one, the one with the books... That's really silly to carry books over there!... anyway, don't forget you have five...

DANIELA: Thank God, Elvis!

Lights on ELVIS waving.

MARCELA: He's going to give me a heart attack... Last month he came home from that demonstration... his clothes in a mess... limping... his video camera broken... his leg injured...

ELVIS: Hey, sis, what's up?! Are you happy? You're gonna FLY over the ocean!

DANIELA: I'll send you a new video camera...

ELVIS: C'mon. That's not what has to be on your mind right now. You're gonna be a Mrs.!!!... May I help you with your luggage Mrs. Aronson...

DANIELA: Daniela Aronson...

MARCELA (*standing up*): Stop these childish games! Hurry. We'll miss the plane.

ELVIS: We? It's just Daniela who's flying. The sky is waiting for you, Mrs. Aronson!

DANIELA: I'm gonna miss this sky...

MARCELA (*sitting down*): You are both completely impractical. Poets! Taking after your father. Listen to me, girl: you have FIVE suitcases: the brown one, the dark blue one, the green one, the one with books, and your backpack, which you'll have with you, ON the plane...

ELVIS and DANIELA look at each other, shaking their heads like "she's never gonna change."

DANIELA walks downstage, carrying one of the suitcases.

DANIELA (*to the audience*): Six. No wedding and a funeral. The BEGINNING!

On the screen is written:

6. NO WEDDING AND A FUNERAL (THE BEGINNING)

February 13, 2001: New York

CHARLIE, GLORIA, and DANIELA, dressed in black, enter CHARLIE's apartment after Mrs. Aronson's funeral.

GLORIA *looks elegant and stylish, wearing a big black - and-white hat. She holds a bottle of red wine, a leftover from Mrs. Aronson's alms. DANIELA carries the suitcase from the previous scene.*

The living room is a mess: papers; four or five laptops; computer monitors; empty cans; used plastic plates, forks, knives, etc. have taken over the place.

GLORIA: This is the messiest mess I've seen in years! You surely know how to welcome guests, bro...

DANIELA (*trying to hide her embarrassment*): It was a great funeral... Your mother was a great lady...

CHARLIE: I didn't have time to / really...

GLORIA: Of course you didn't. Old-fashioned time oppressing our busy e-genius! (*to DANIELA*) That was always his excuse, and Mom would rush to clean up the mess for her sweet brilliant perfect little Charley...

CHARLIE: You can leave the wine in the kitchen.

GLORIA (*she doesn't move*): Perfect spoiled little Charley!

Awkward silence. DANIELA feels the need to do or say

something. She starts picking up the cans, etc.

DANIELA: I can clean up... No problem... (*to*

CHARLIE) Are you going to work tomorrow

morning?

CHARLIE: I must.

GLORIA (*to DANIELA*): You must not! You are not

paid as a cleaning lady! (*to CHARLIE*) Did you have

her clean Mom's house?

DANIELA: Oh, no. Mrs. Aronson did everything by

herself. She was so energetic! (*tidying the room*) So

kind... She used to say that retirement made her

stronger than ever... "I don't need help anymore, girl!

Anna, the cleaning lady, comes here only once a

month. To play pinochle with me!"

GLORIA: That's Mom... Her own big heart killing her

in the end...

CHARLIE takes off his shoes. He wears white socks. He

turns a laptop on.

GLORIA: Here he is. Mr. Laptop! Mr. I-don't-care-

lemme-alone-go-fuck-yourself. (*to DANIELA)* We

don't exist for him. (*She hands the bottle of wine to DANIELA.*) I'm out of here, honey... Good luck!

GLORIA walks up stage. Lights fade on her.

DANIELA (*to CHARLIE*): Are you all right? Do you need anything?

CHARLIE: A bagel with ham and cream cheese, thanks.

DANIELA: Sure!

CHARLIE: If there are any bagels left in the fridge.

DANIELA: Oh.

CHARLIE: Did Gloria leave for good? (*looks at her*) You can put that wine in the kitchen...

DANIELA (*doesn't move*): Gloria is such a nice person... She's an artist, isn't she?

CHARLIE: Yeah, she's the artist in the family.

DANIELA: One can tell...

She heads to the kitchen.

CHARLIE: Oh, no!

DANIELA: I didn't mean / to say...

CHARLIE: I ate the last bagel this morning.

DANIELA: I can go and buy some! I feel like Christmas every time I enter a shop here in New York. There are so many products. I like taking everything and putting it in my bag! I have never seen so many types of bread, of cheese, of bagels! Whole wheat, blueberry, onion, garlic, cinnamon raisin, sourdough, sesame seed, pumpernickel, poppy seed, everything /...

CHARLIE: I like the plain ones.

DANIELA: I can buy plain.

CHARLIE: You need cash, don't you? (*checks his wallet*)

DANIELA (*nodding*): I don't know how to use your credit cards. We didn't have such things. But I'm gonna learn!

CHARLIE: I'm out of cash... There's some meat in the freezer. Can you cook?

DANIELA: Cook?

CHARLIE: I've never had Romanian food. Can you prepare something Romanian?

DANIELA: Romanian? Yes, but... I don't / really...

CHARLIE: Mom was a good cook.

DANIELA (*beat*): I can try.

She goes up stage, to the "kitchen." She comes back in a second.

DANIELA (*excited*): May I use the microwave?

CHARLIE: You'll only need the stove.

DANIELA's enthusiasm evaporates. She walks downstage.

DANIELA (*to the audience*): Seven. Goodbye, America. Another end.

On the screen is written:

7. GOOD BYE, AMERICA! (ANOTHER END)

August 23, 2001: New York

A subway station. Noises of trains passing. Noises of people waiting. UROS lies on four seats, apparently asleep. There is a small radio at his head playing some soft music. DANIELA looks anxious. CEAUŞESCU and ELENA, dressed up, follow her. She rushes to UROS, talking fast.

DANIELA: Hey Uros... Wake up!...

ELENA (*mockingly*): Wake up! Wake up!

DANIELA: I have good news... I got the money... I have your ticket for Iraq!... Good bye, America!... I bought a one-way ticket for me too... I'm going back... My flight is at eleven am, yours is at eleven-thirty am... We can travel together to the airport... we'll take a cab!... I managed to use his MasterCard, I finally learned how to use their damn credit cards... Uros!?... You'll go to Iraq, you'll find your soul, your... "immortality"!

ELENA: Isn't she deadly stupid?

DANIELA: What can I do?! Back to hairy tales... Charlie loves his laptops and his plain bagels, not me... He needs a good cook, not me... Small word this "love"! In Romanian is bigger: "dragoste"... Uros?!... Talk to me...

ELENA (*mockingly*): Talk to her!

DANIELA: Uros? ...

CEAUŞESCU: Leave him alone, comrade!

DANIELA: ...You know what... I'm not sure of this going back... Mom will have a heart attack... she tells every neighbor and his uncle ... everyone in the elevator, in the peasant's market, all the saleswomen in the supermarket know how HAPPY I am with my American husband... Charlie is not my husband!... C'mon, Uros, (*laughing*) I know you tried to sell him his own tie... I'm not angry at you... Uros?!... Uros?!... (*beat*) You're not dead, are you?... No... No!

CEAUȘESCU and ELENA: Cheers!

DANIELA (*to UROS*): Don't do this to me, Uros... Don't... Don't... We have plane tickets! (*She freezes for a while, then turns off the radio, gets up, takes the radio.*) I'll give it back to Charlie...

ELENA: Weak-Spot-of-the-Second-Degree: HIT. Weak-Spot-of-the-First-Degree: TO BE DETECTED. Cheers!

CEAUȘESCU: You are a genius!

DANIELA *walks downstage. Funeral music.*

CEAUȘESCU *and ELENA dance, laughing.*

DANIELA: Last nightmare for this evening...

ELENA: Cheers!

CEAUȘESCU: Noroc!

On the screen is written:

8. LAST NIGHTMARE (FOR THIS EVENING)

The party of dead people. They all have long hair, hairy arms, legs, faces, etc. They all smile. Big smiles. Fake smiles. Sick smiles. Condescending smiles. All sorts of smiles. They drink red wine and chat like at any reception. (The scene can be played without any of the above, just with CEAUŞESCU and ELENA in the "party mood")

DANIELA (*to the audience*): "Don't laugh at other people's dreams or nightmares" —I read this in "Introduction to Chinese Wisdom." It's not a stolen book. I found it in the trash, on our street. I had to take it home! This is how I learned that I was born in the Year of the Horse / ...One can find so many great things in the garbage here, in New York.

CEAUŞESCU: Shut up, horse!

DANIELA: It's like they wait for us there, in the rubbish, feeling sad, lonely, and rejected...

ELENA kicks DANIELA and forces her to get on her knees.

ELENA: On! On! Move on, pig!

CEAUȘESCU: Horse. She's a horse.

ELENA: Whatever.

CEAUȘESCU: We shouldn't have taken her here. Everybody left their pets at the door.

ELENA: She's not a pet. She's a servant.

CEAUȘESCU: She's our horse. Our dog. Our rat. Our darling little guinea pig. And our cook, of course.

ELENA: Our cleaning girl.

CEAUȘESCU: Your waxing lady.

ELENA: I've got so hairy now that I'm dead. Why does hair grow on dead people? Look: everybody is so hairy around here.

CEAUȘESCU: Let's not ruin our mood for the sake of hair!

They take two glasses of red wine and drink with relish.

ELENA: To … forever!

CEAUȘESCU: To… Draculand!

ELENA: You mean Disneyland.

CEAUȘESCU: Not at all. We'll have our own park! They're building Draculand in Transylvania, near Sighisoara.

ELENA: You didn't tell me!

CEAUŞESCU: Look, the girl...

ELENA: The horse?

CEAUŞESCU: She's not smiling. Everyone else is smiling. She's not. She's thinking!

ELENA: Oh, no. You think, pig?

CEAUŞESCU: Yes, she is. I can tell by the wrinkles on her forehead.

ELENA: Let's hear that! Think louder, horse!.... What are you waiting for?... I said, THINK, pig!

She kicks DANIELA.

DANIELA: Given the existence of something beyond existence, I have ceased to exist.

She starts licking CEAUŞESCU's hand.

DANIELA: I am your ashtray. Your tomb. Your Disneyland. Your past. Your present. Your future. You can do with me whatever you want. I am here to stay. I am here to endure. I am here to live...

CEAUŞESCU: She's sick!

ELENA: Enough, pet! Wait in front of the door!

DANIELA: Ruins. I'm an earthworm crawling among wrecks. Eating the dust... (*She starts licking ELENA's hand.*)

CEAUȘESCU: Send her home! She'll ruin our party...

DANIELA: Dust. Rust. Blood. Champagne. Wedding. Funeral. Birth. Death. Cut. Grow. Wax. Grow. Hair. Hair. Hair. Everywhere. Hair!

ELENA kicks DANIELA's back. CEAUȘESCU pats it, like he'd do with a horse.

ELENA: Vanish from my gaze! ...Fuck off!

CEAUȘESCU: Leave us alone!

DANIELA is crawling left stage.

ELENA: I hate her. She's too... too... unusual!

CEAUȘESCU (*fondling her hand*): Forget her. Let's talk about us. Let's talk about love!

ELENA: You turned into a boring romantic vampire. You're far below your reputation. Dracula was... well... he was somebody.

CEAUȘESCU: Stop comparing me with the myth... I grew to like some anonymity. Just you and me in a little house, somewhere in the forest...

ELENA: How boring.

CEAUȘESCU: Just you and me on a beach. Listening to the ocean...

ELENA: You're not yourself. You shouldn't drink red wine. It softens you.

CEAUȘESCU: Just you and me, biting and devouring each other...

ELENA: This sounds much better...

They start caressing and kissing their necks. The party guests applaud. They surround them. Cheer them.

CEAUȘESCU and ELENA devour each other... It takes a while...

SONG

CEAUȘESCU: CHEERS, MY LOVE! CHEERS!

LET ME EAT YOUR EARS!

ELENA: OH, GIVE ME A PECK

LET ME GRIP YOUR NECK!

CEAUȘESCU and ELENA:

(refrain)

LET ME BE YOUR COOK

LET ME THRUST MY HOOK

LET ME TASTE YOUR VEINS

LET ME KEEP YOUR REINS

LET ME CATCH YOUR FLU

LET ME BE YOUR STEW

TU, TU, TU, TU (*'you' in Romanian, pronounced 'tou'*)

LET ME HAVE A BITE

OF YOU!

CEAUŞESCU: YOUR BREAST IS STILL SO FRESH

I LOVE TO CHOMP YOUR FLESH

ELENA: YOUR EYES TASTE LIKE A RADISH

THEY'RE STILL MY FAVORITE DISH

CEAUŞESCU: YOUR HEART IS PLAIN AND HARD

A VIBRANT BUSINESS CARD

ELENA: YOUR BRAIN IS A BIT BITTER

YOUR NEURONS STILL GLITTER

CEAUȘESCU and ELENA:

(*refrain*)

LET ME BE YOUR COOK

LET ME THRUST MY HOOK

LET ME TASTE YOUR VEINS

LET ME KEEP YOUR REINS

LET ME CATCH YOUR FLU

LET ME BE YOUR STEW

TU, TU, TU, TU

CEAUȘESCU: YOUR LEGS ARE HOME-BAKED

PIES

THEY'RE NOT FOR FOREIGN SPIES!

ELENA: DON'T GET DRUNK ON MY BLOOD

LIKE A CAPITALIST STUD!

CEAUȘESCU: BITE ME, CHEW ME, CHOMP ME

YOU WON'T HEAR ANY SOB

HISTORY BOOKS CAN TELL YOU

I'M NOT TO PLEASE THE MOB!

ELENA: FRY ME, GRILL ME, BURN ME

YOU WON'T HEAR ANY SOB

HISTORY BOOKS CAN TELL YOU

I'M NOT TO PLEASE THE MOB!

They fall on the floor, exhausted.

DANIELA: Cheers! Red wine and white sheets.

Gloria's bedroom. Nine.

On the screen is written:

9. RED WINE AND WHITE SHEETS

August 25, 2001: New York

DANIELA is in bed, drunk, fully covered with sheets, in GLORIA's apartment. GLORIA walks back and forth downstage.

GLORIA: You cannot do this. This is not something that can be done.

DANIELA: I'm sorry, Gloria... I didn't mean to...

GLORIA (*mimicking her*): I'm sorry, I'm sorry... Who cares if you're sorry or not. The issue is you're... crazy! Silly. Dumb. Mean. All of them!

DANIELA: I just wanted to...

GLORIA: Fuck!

DANIELA: ...talk to somebody...

GLORIA: Right. You come here, drink my wine, eat my lasagna, laugh at my jokes, nod at my words of wisdom, dance Greek, get naked, jump into my bed, and when I finally put my hand on your ass, you start crying on my tits, like a screaming brat, a baby, that you cannot do this, you cannot do this... oh, poor girl, oh sweet innocent girl... gimme a fucking break!

DANIELA (*tipsy*): I don't know...

GLORIA: You don't know!... You know what, honey, doll, pussycat: you should start learning to make some choices, some decisions... Your own decisions. What do you actually want? Me? Charlie? Maybe you need your mom to tell you what to do, ask her for permission for... everything: permission to move, to breathe, to drink, to eat, to fuck, to live, so you wouldn't have to think too hard...

DANIELA: I think a lot... a great deal...

GLORIA: Well, show me a tiny corner of the outcome of this great thinking process...

DANIELA: ...my head is so... full of... shit... thoughts... I don't know... worms in my brain... biting... biting... you know... ghosts...

GLORIA (*sits down on the bed and starts massaging DANIELA's temples, motherly*): Life is too damn short and tense, Daniela... it frowns and snaps at us everyday... let's give it a big smile in exchange, a big "cheers"!... let's tell her: you won't kick me down, bitch, you won't... Let's relax, forget about worries... to the garbage with the past!... welcome the present... the moment... stop it in your lap... stroke it... rub it... the moment is yours... enjoy it... award yourself with some good time... we deserve it... you deserve it...

She kisses DANIELA who doesn't respond.

Blackout.

DANIELA (*to the audience*): Sorry. I'm not gonna tell you what happened. (*whispering*) Make up your own stories!... (*informal tone*) Okay. I can tell you something. I was strong. I made a decision. I did it MY way.

Lights on.

DANIELA: Okay. We have to move on. That's it. Time doesn't actually stop. Stop! Stop! See, it doesn't...

Ten! In the long run.

On the screen is written:

10. IN THE LONG RUN

September 11, 2001: New York

CHARLIE's apartment. DANIELA and CHARLIE, drink their coffee standing and moving around the room.

CHARLIE: I cannot come with you to the airport.

DANIELA: I'll take a cab.

CHARLIE: Are you sure?

DANIELA: Yes, I'll take a cab.

CHARLIE: About leaving.

DANIELA: I cannot waste the money for the plane ticket, can I?

CHARLIE: It's my money.

DANIELA: That's why. It's the money I stole...

CHARLIE: I don't wanna talk about money.

DANIELA: Sure.

CHARLIE: Are you sure? About leaving.

DANIELA: I don't know...

CHARLIE: Don't you have everything you need? New York, free time, good food, nice clothes? Shelves full of products? "Like Christmas everyday"?!

DANIELA: I don't know...

CHARLIE: Who knows then?

DANIELA (*beat*): You don't love me.

Lights on CEAUŞESCU and ELENA. They look worn out but take pleasure in mocking DANIELA.

CEAUŞESCU and ELENA: Love me! Marry me!

DANIELA (*to CHARLIE*): You don't need me.

CEAUŞESCU and ELENA: Love me! Marry me!

They go on whispering "love me, marry me," mockingly.

DANIELA: You won't marry me.

CHARLIE (*beat, then outburst*): I never wished to get married! I didn't want all that shit: two-story house, two cars, two kids, two dogs, weekends with the family. Fake communication. Fake smiles. Social convention... A cheap Hollywood movie!... A computer game is more entertaining than this old (*grinning*) "Happy Family" game... Mom used to play it so well... (*beat*) I don't like being like everybody else!

DANIELA: What about your sister? She's not like everybody else. Nobody is like everybody else.

CHARLIE: Gloria! Mrs. "I don't care but let's pretend I do"... I hope you didn't fuck her...

DANIELA: Who cares if I did?

CHARLIE: Did you?

DANIELA: You have a real problem with women, Charlie!

CHARLIE: Sure. Right. I hate the American self-righteous women. The Latino over-talkative chicks.

The British snobbish giraffes. The French sexy inflatable dolls. The Asian midget mistresses...

DANIELA: What is this, the anti-women manifesto?

CHARLIE: I didn't want a female pet from a third-world country...

DANIELA: Thanks a lot!

CHARLIE: I'm not talking about you. It's the big screen! The big picture. Can't you see it? Same rules of the game. Same score. Same music. Work, eat, fuck, work, eat, fuck... Bed, job, kitchen, bed, job, kitchen...

DANIELA: You said enough...

DANIELA goes up stage to the "kitchen." CEAUŞESCU and ELENA follow her and remain there.

CHARLIE (*in lower voice*): I'm okay with you though...

DANIELA: You're a selfish /... robot, Charlie!

CHARLIE: I'm okay with you...

DANIELA comes back to the living room.

DANIELA: Mrs. Aronson told me you were kind, smart, sweet, tender, funny, generous, gentle, well-behaved, polite, loving, lovable, SPECIAL!

CHARLIE doesn't look at her.

CHARLIE: Yeah, Mom believed I was different. Special. Very special... "There, above the TV set, I'm gonna hang your Nobel Prize!"... Sure, Mom... "Computers are the future, and you're a genius of computers!... Well, Mom... "Here, look at this photo, a nice decent girl from Romania, to take care of you... after I'll be gone." That's silly, Mom... "You'll thank me for this, Charley, you'll see, you will..." Sure, Mom... Nothing about music, everything about disk drives and devices with removable storage... "You're great at violin, Charley, but violin is like a vampire, it softens you, it makes you suffer, squeak, and sob all day long. This is not a life for you, Charley!"... THIS is surely not a life, Mom...

DANIELA is clearly moved by his monologue but doesn't know what to do: to show her emotion or to still be angry with him. Lights fade on CHARLIE.

DANIELA (*to the audience*): I'm trying to imagine him playing the violin... (*beat, she's listening the air*) I can't. There's no violin sound that I can associate with him. Only keyboard clicks. Click click click. Click click

click... Wait a minute! (*A violin can be heard louder and louder.*)

DANIELA stares tenderly at CHARLIE—she realizes she cares about him.

ELENA: Weak-Spot-of-the-First-Degree: DETECTED.

ALL: Eleven!

On the screen:

9/11. FLASH BACK, FLASH FORWARD.

DANIELA packs her last things. Two big suitcases are already ready to go. From time to time she stops packing, and freezes for awhile in a meditative position. Same violin music, softly played.

DANIELA: Two suitcases: the big brown one and the heavy black one... One with clothes and presents. One with books... Ah, and the small red bag that I'm going to keep with me on the plane... That means THREE... Okay. What's wrong now? Bye-bye, New York, that's all... (*violin music goes louder*) Does it make any sense? I mean this thing that sometimes, after years, or weeks, or days, or hours, or just seconds, boom, a thunderstorm hits your mind and you begin to catch the other one's thoughts, you begin to understand, to see, to hear, all of a sudden, the music locked inside his body... and you can't stop listening... you can't stop...

Lights on CEAUȘESCU and ELENA who start sniffing DANIELA. Violin music stops. Lights on the other actors.

DANIELA (*continuing*): Okay. I have three suitcases... The big brown one... the heavy black one...

CEAUȘESCU: I can smell the blood in the air...

ELENA: The pain...

CEAUȘESCU: Same smell...

ELENA: And growing!

DANIELA: Running...

CEAUȘESCU: The crowd is mad at us.

ELENA: Worms. Crush them!

CEAUȘESCU: Shoot them!

DANIELA: I'm stumbling...

MARCELA: We don't want your future husband to think we're dirty!

ELVIS: Run, Dani, run!

DANIELA: A fresh corpse at my feet...

ELVIS: Don't look down. Look at the sky...

DANIELA: Bodies....

CEAUŞESCU: She sees our helicopter taking off from the roof of the palace!

DANIELA: Smashed.

ELENA: She stops!

DANIELA: Crushed.

ELENA: Pointing with her forefinger

CEAUŞESCU: at us!

ELENA: Shouting like a starved pussy cat.

DANIELA: The dictator is leaving!

ELVIS: The crowd is screaming...

CEAUŞESCU: "Don't let them leave!"...

ELENA: "Don't let them... live!"

DANIELA: Live!

ELVIS: In Bucharest.

MARCELA: In New York!

ELVIS: Watching on TV how they kill them

MARCELA: on Christmas night!

DANIELA: A quick trial

CEAUŞESCU: I don't accept this court!

ELENA: Who is the judge?

CEAUŞESCU: I am the President of the Socialist Republic of Romania and I shall answer only before the Grand National Assembly and before representatives of the working class and that is all, I've finished!

DANIELA, MARCELA, and ELVIS: Guilty!

ELENA: What a provocation!

ELVIS: They shoot *Ceauşescu* and Elena

ELENA: They shoot US!

DANIELA: He-Comrade and She-Comrade are

CEAUŞESCU and ELENA: Dead...

ELVIS: Punished

MARCELA: A Christmas present

DANIELA: for the Romanian people

ELENA: Stupid murderers. Wooden heads. Vampires!

CEAUŞESCU (*whispering*): It's not them, it's the foreign agencies...

ELENA: It hurts!

DANIELA: To be guilty or

GLORIA: Not guilty!

CEAUŞESCU and ELENA: Who is the judge?

ELVIS: The sky

GLORIA: The sky

ELVIS: The helicopter

GLORIA: The plane

DANIELA: One cannot escape

GLORIA: One can escape

MARCELA: My son-in-law is a businessman! In New York!

GLORIA: The towers

DANIELA: The walls

ELVIS: The dreams

CEAUŞESCU: The golden dream of communism!

GLORIA: Burning. Melting.

DANIELA: Crumbling

ELVIS: Watching on TV

MARCELA: A nightmare!

GLORIA: The choreography of death

DANIELA: One cannot escape. Pain speaks all languages.

ELVIS: Run, Dani, run!

GLORIA: Run, Charlie, run! /

MARCELA: Run, Daniela, run!

UROS: Run, girl!

DANIELA: Run, Charlie, / run!

GLORIA: Run!

ELVIS: Run!

MARCELA: Run!

UROS: Run!

DANIELA: AGAIN?

GLORIA, MARCELA, and ELVIS: Run!

DANIELA: Where?

GLORIA: Here.

ELVIS: Fire

DANIELA: Sweat

CEAUŞESCU: Blood

MARCELA: Money

GLORIA: Bodies

DANIELA: Hair

GLORIA: Hands

ELVIS: Legs

DANIELA: Thighs

GLORIA: Hips

ELENA: Buttocks

CEAUŞESCU: Demolition

ELENA: Mutilation

UROS: Death

DANIELA: Love!

GLORIA: Loss

MARCELA: Business!

ELVIS: Hope

CEAUŞESCU: The golden future!

GLORIA: The present...

DANIELA: The past, always the past...

CEAUŞESCU, ELENA, MARCELA, ELVIS, GLORIA, and UROS: Guilty!

DANIELA: Stop this! I've had enough of this! Enough!

(*The other characters start pushing and pulling DANIELA in different directions, she gets rid of them.*)

I haven't done anything wrong. I don't owe anything to you... I'm rather owed some good normal boring times... Like everybody else... You, ghosts, have waxed the soul out of me. But you know what: there's still something left. A tiny little piece of me. See?! I'm hairy but not dead...

(*She tears up the plane ticket, violin music is played.*)

I can hear! I can hear you playing the violin, Charlie. Yes, I do. I'm sure. Yes. You will come home. You will find me here. We'll talk. And I won't say "I'm sorry." I will say: let's start again! This melodramatic incredible impractical improbable... hairy-tale.

Violin music resumes. On the screen is written: **END/BEGINNING.** *Daniela takes Charlie's photo out of her pajama's pocket and shows it nervously to the spectators:*

DANIELA: Have you seen him? Charlie Aronson. Blue eyes, brown hair. Age thirty-eight. He worked at the sixty-sixth floor. Yes, I'm sure he managed to get down. He's smart. Not very talkative, but smart. Charlie. Charlie Aronson. Do you know him? He liked to play the violin... Yes, he's tall. Like an oak grown by the sun, thin like a barbed wire, silent like a fish and blind like a jellyfish... I'm joking. These are our jokes... Have you seen him? Charlie. This is the photo his mom sent to my mom. It's a photo taken on his birthday. He looks so sad, doesn't he? Charlie Aronson. He's wearing a white shirt and a brown tie with purple circles. He has a silver watch. Yes. On his left hand. And silly white socks. Yes, white. Do you know him?... Do you?... Do you?

Lights fade. The violin music grows louder and louder, filling the whole space.

End/beginning.

LENIN'S SHOE

CHARACTERS:

IVAN IVANOVICH (Vanya), 58, Russian-American

VLADIMIR IVANOVICH (Vlad), 16, his son, in a wheelchair.

IRINA LENKIN, 21, waitress/student.

JASNA DURIC, 37, Romanian-Macedonian-Bosnian, Vlad's tutor.

ALEX DURIC, 17, Jasna's son.

HASSAN DURIC, 42, Jasna's husband, Bosnian

KEBAB, 28, homeless.

PLACE: A house in QUEENS, New York.

The ground floor is the restaurant "Uncle Vanya" and the first floor is the owner's home.

TIME: December, 2003

/ - marks the moment of interruption in overlapping dialogue

ACT I

Scene 1

Morning. Vlady's room.

There's not much furniture but many books and shoes.

He's immersed in his computer, wearing headphones.

Vlady's blog: LONERS' PARTY

VLADY: Abandon Hope and Stupidity, All Ye Who enter this Blog! Exclamation mark. Working title: Loners' Party. Party like in Communist Party. Or Party like in Christmas party. Birthday party. Wedding party. Whatever pops into your mind when you say "party" (-: Smiley face.

 "Scared nurse" party. Scared the shit out of her. Cut my face a tiny little bit and there she was, screaming and weeping, real tears, I swear. Silly nurses he brings to me, always silly nurses. Desperate immigrants. Telenovela characters called Maria. The one before this Columbian Mariella was a Romanian called Mariana. She had huge tits and a dream to marry an American millionaire. She might lie on a beach in

Hawaii right now. He kicked her out after I cut my veins and drew huge breasts in blood on the walls.

The one before the Romanian was Polish. Very religious. She had like twenty crosses and icons with the poor Christ crucified on wood and metal and silver and gold and... She left after my attempt to crucify myself on the window.

Let's see who's the next one. I'll prepare fireworks for her, huge fireworks. Smiley face.

Scene 2

The Salon (a room reserved for the owner and his guests in the back of the restaurant).

Jasna enters but no one is there.

VANYA *(shouting offstage):* Misha, Andrei, Olga, where the fuck are you? We have a Christmas Party and a New Year's fucking Party coming up! Misha, throw that cigarette away and get over here you idiot! I brought you here, I got you legal papers so you don't need to hide in dirty basements anymore, and do you show me any gratitude? Selfish morons! Next week in Moscow I'll have Russian begging me for this job, begging me on their knees, crawling for this job!

He enters the Salon and sees Jasna.

VANYA: Yes? Who are you looking for? Do you speak English?

JASNA: Sure. I'm Jasna Duric, I'm here for the job.

VANYA *(he looks at her)*: You're too old for waitress. I need fresh girls for that, you understand.

JASNA: I heard you need a tutor. For your son.

VANYA: Where did you hear that?

JASNA: In the food shop... A woman was just complaining you kicked her out...

VANYA: I didn't kick her out! She left, the stupid old cow. She couldn't do her job. I fired her, I didn't kick her out. I didn't even touch her! *(he looks at Jasna with more attention)* I need a nurse for my son, not a tutor. He goes to school on-line.

JASNA: I can do both, I can be a nurse, I can be a tutor, I can clean the house, / I can do all...

VANYA: What kind of accent is that?

JASNA: Russian-Romanian-Macedonian-Bosnian.

VANYA: Powder-keg! You're a powder-keg.

JASNA: Don't smoke next to me!

VANYA (smiling at the joke but trying to hide it): So you need papers. Legal papers.

JASNA: I have degrees in journalism and Slavic languages.

VANYA: Great. But useless. What's your name?

JASNA: Jasna - "clear" in Russian.

VANYA: Harasho. Let's make things clear Jasna: I have degrees in literature and philosophy and... here we are! You like my restaurant, my "Uncle Vanya"?

JASNA: It's great. Very Chekovian. In a good way, I mean.

(she takes a paper out of her purse)

VANYA: It's the best in Queens. And next year I'm opening one in Manhattan. On Wall Street. What's that?

JASNA: My CV.

(she hands it to him)

VANYA: CV?! You're really funny. Take a seat! (she doesn't; he's reading her CV) War correspondent?! Why should I hire you, to report on what? I'm not at war with my son!

JASNA: See, I have teaching experience. And I have a son too. I'm really good with the young men.

VANYA *(flirting):* And how good are you with "old" men like me? *(he takes a bottle of vodka from under the table, pours vodka in two glasses and gives her one)* War correspondent... I drink for you, Jasna. You're a survivor. Cheers! To life! What's life, Jasna, but a pathetic fight for survival? Dog eats dog. Man kills man. Dog and man kill cat. Cat eats mouse. And we all eat cheese! *(he laughs like he made a great joke)* Life is nothing but cartoons, Jasna. *(he drinks)*

JASNA: Are you giving me the job?

VANYA: You wanna play the Mary Poppins role?

JASNA: People say I look like Julie Andrews.

VANYA: And you believe them?

JASNA: Try me on your son!

VANYA: Vladimir is a special boy. A bit crazy after the accident.

JASNA: What accident?

VANYA: Let's just call it "the accident". Since then Vlady tried – or pretended to try - to commit suicide 113 times. Yeah, that's a pretty tough record, isn't it?

JASNA: Why don't you send him to a hospital, to an... asylum?

VANYA: I'm not gonna send my only child to an asylum! That was a silly thing to say, Jasna. There's nothing wrong with Vlady's brain. *(he drinks)* He's just a bit rebellious, that's all...

JASNA: I know what you mean, my Alex is a rebel without a cause too....He's 17.

VANYA *(he pours vodka in her glass, flirtatious)*: When did you have him, in the sixth grade? And what about your husband, the "pedophile"?

JASNA: Hassan. Poet Laureate at Struga in Macedonia. First Muslim Bosnian to get the big award... *(she drinks the glass of vodka in one shot)*

VANYA: I bet he doesn't get any big awards here...

JASNA: Are you hiring me or not?

VANYA: You can't handle a crippled boy, Jasna.

JASNA: Oh, yes, I can! It's normal people that I can't handle anymore. I feel like shouting in their face: hey, there are people dying out there and you're eating calmly your fucking pizza in front of your stupid TV!

VANYA: Don't get angry, Jasna, you're not pretty when you get angry!

JASNA: Do I need to be pretty for this job?

VANYA: Look, Jasna, I hired only simple women for this job. This is it. I don't need over-educated women who'd grow frustrated, bitter and angry on life. I've got enough drama... *(shaking his glass with vodka)* Lucky me, I also have the Russian shrink - Dr Stolichnaya!

JASNA: Maybe an over-educated woman is exactly what your son needs. A tutor not a nurse. Let me talk with the boy!

VANYA: You're stubborn, Jasna... OK, let's pay Vlady a visit. *(she smiles)* Yes! When you smile, your eyes kinda dance, kinda sing, you look a bit like that Julie Andrews...

Scene 3

Vlady's bedroom. Lots of shoes with no shoe-laces are neatly placed on the floor, almost filling the room. VANYA and JASNA enter.

Vlady doesn't look at them. He's in a wheelchair.

VLADY: you wanna see that murda murda

it's murda murda!... /

(he goes on and on rapping over Vanya's lines)

Murdaa I-N-C

Nigga know the rule I be

The kinda nigga you see

Mug shot 6 o'clock TV

Spit off 3

J to the A-R-U-L-E

Murdaa MIB

VANYA: Hey, man, let me introduce you to a nice lady! Vlad, I want you to meet somebody! Vlad. Vladimir!

VLADY: you wanna see that murda murda

it's murda murda

We live it.. we breathe it.. we screamin' murda

VANYA *(to Jasna):* His new passion: 'gansta hip-hop'.
A bunch of black guys with weird names: Ja Rule, 50
Cents... He googles them on the internet... Am I right,
aren't you googling everything, Vlad? ... Any 'One
Dollar' rap star coming up?...

VLADY *(to Jasna):* Do you wanna hear a piece from
my album 'Hail, Mamma Russia goes to jail!'

VANYA: I don't think she does, Vladimir.

JASNA: I actually do.

VANYA *(to Jasna):* You don't want to encourage him
on that. *(to Vlady)* Vlad, I'm leaving for Russia next
week. I need to find a new nurse for you. Tomorrow
and the day after tomorrow you'll get to see a bunch
of candidates. Try to behave!

VLADY: go to jail, mamma

yo, go to jail

you need a rest, mamma

from this hell

everything sucks, mamma

we screamin': boooo

yo, booooo

I ain't asked, mamma

to be born to you!

Who shots you?!

JASNA *(to Vlady):* This is something you wrote? Very

good!

VLADY: You don't need to gimme strawberry shit,

man, all right?

VANYA: Vlad, she's Jasna...

VLADY *(to Jasna):* You don't look like a nurse... The

last one we had smelled like an ambulant hospital.

Yo! This is a treat, man. You're a hot chick! Yo!

VANYA: Watch your mouth, Vladimir!

JASNA: It's OK. It's been a while since I was called a

hot chick.

VANYA: Vladimir Ivanovich, I want to hear you

articulating complete sentences from now on.

Understand? *(to Jasna)* He enjoys acting like a

monkey.

VLADY: Mo-mo-mo-mo-monkey...

Do-do-do-do-donkey...

VANYA (to Jasna): He likes to push my limits. (he looks at his watch)

VLADY: Yes, sir, comrade Ivan! Pioneer Vladimir Ivanovich at your orders! I promise to articulate complete phrases. Human sentences. I will execute the red monkey abiding in my brain. Mo-mo-mo-mo! Chop her head off. Scoop her brain out and serve it up, for you only, sir, our special Japanese-Russian-American-Human-Animal delicatessen! Mo-mo-mo-mo! Ka-ka-ka-ka!

VANYA: Enough! *(to Jasna)* There's no point in talking with him. Let's go!

JASNA: I'd like to stay a few more minutes. / I just...

VANYA: Five minutes. *(leaving the room)* Make him call me daddy!

Vanya leaves.

VLADY *(mockingly)*: Ha, ha, ha. He thinks he's funny...

JASNA: You think you're funny too...

VLADY: I ain't funny, man. I ain't pretty, I suck, I ain't fit, I killed ma luck. I wanna be black! Niga !

JASNA: Okay. Black is good. Can we have a normal conversation now. A normal boring conversation.

VLADY: Bore me to death, nurse. Teach me how to swim, sista. Murda me!

JASNA: C'mon Vlad. He's gone. You don't have to impress him anymore.

VLADY: Whadda ya wanna hear?

JASNA (looking around the room): I've never seen a room with so many shoes. There are like – how many – 80 pairs? What's this, the shoes' army, Vladenka?

VLADY: Didn't the Motherfucker tell you the funny and tragic shoe-story, man? You know, shoooo, boooom!

JASNA: Shoe-story?

VLADY: Shoo, nigga! I got knocked out by a shoe. But that don't allow you to gimme any pink strawberry shit, yo. I mean no funny pity-looks, all right. We're clear on that? Jasna?

JASNA: I don't pity you, Vlad. I think you're very talented. And brave. And handsome / and…

VLADY: Fuck off! I'm not your fucking charity case, yo!

JASNA: OK, OK. What kinda person you want to take care of you?

VLADY: You wanna take care of me? Suck my dick when my dick get hard!

JASNA: Hey. I didn't hear that! *(beat)* So you have your computer. You have lot of music. Do you like to read?

VLADY: I stare at the window.

JASNA *(going to the window)*: Not much to see. The restaurant is underneath, right?

VLADY: Uncle Vanya, a stupid fucking name for a restaurant. Just to fucking look well-read. *(beat)* Where are you from, nigga?

JASNA: Romania, Bosnia... Macedonia.

VLADY: Macedonia! That was a great country like 2000, 3000 years ago...

JASNA: You learn all these things on-line?

VLADY: Self-taught, man. All I need is right here...
(he goes to the window) Are we done with this
"interview"?

JASNA: No. Here's another question for you: What
do you do when you go out?

VLADY*(beat)*: I don't leave this fucking room, man...

JASNA: Never?

VLADY: Look. Out there, in the street, leaning against
that dumpster. *(lights up on Kebab)* See that guy? The
dark guy. Waiting for leftovers from our "Uncle
Vanya"... Look at him. Frying in his own sauce on the
asphalt-pan... I call him 'Kebab'... He's got that
look...

JASNA *(looking out the window)*: The "kebab" look?

VLADY: Yo, woman. It's THE look. The murda-look.
We're brothers!

Scene 4

*The Salon. Vanya sits at the table with the head in his
hands. Jasna enters.*

VANYA: You're hired, Jasna. Go home and pack! Be back tomorrow morning at 6 am. I'm leaving for Russia tomorrow night. You'll take care of the house here.

JASNA: Great but... When are you coming back?

VANYA: I'll bring you a golden necklace to wear at the New Year's party!

JASNA: We didn't talk about my weekends off.

VANYA: No weekends off. It's a full-time job.

JASNA: But I have a son, I have responsibilities...

VANYA: $500 a week.

JASNA: No woman would work without at least one day off!

VANYA: You'd be surprised....

JASNA: You don't have time to interview other women.

VANYA: $600.

JASNA: I need the Sundays off.

VANYA: Sundays off - after I'm back.

JASNA: Why can't you leave after Christmas?

VANYA: It's business.

JASNA: What business, nobody cares about business in Russia, in Eastern Europe, on Christmas' Eve...

VANYA: 650 – last offer.

JASNA: 700.

VANYA: 650 - And I'll help you with the green-card.

JASNA: I'll be here tomorrow morning.

VANYA: I love you, Jasna!

Scene 5

Lights shift to a shabby kitchen in Ridgewood, Queens. Evening.

Jasna sets the table for three, listening to NPR. Hassan enters.

HASSAN: Kalate radio!

JASNA: English!

HASSAN: Need listen that? Why listen that, woman? *(he pushes STOP)*

JASNA: I got a well paid job, Hassan! 650 dollars a week! I just have to take care of a crippled Russian boy. And to live there, in-house. His father is the owner of that restaurant Uncle Vanya.

HASSAN: What? You will no here nights? No see you anymore? Like we no husband and wife! Alex will problem!

JASNA: But we're gonna have money, we can start living, Hassan! I'm so tired of being poor, I'm tired of hitting the same wall again and again. I want to start living!

HASSAN: Start living? With the Russians? You have son, you have husband!

JASNA: You can take care of the boy when I'm not here. You're at home almost all the time. You haven't got a trip with the limo in weeks!

HASSAN: I got today. Julia Roberts.

JASNA: What?

HASSAN: I have Julia Roberts in limo.

JASNA: What are you talking about?

HASSAN: Julia in limo. Sexy. Beautiful. Smile. Big smile. Dress like TV. I take Julia at the airport. I take Julia at big big house at Connecticut.

JASNA: No kidding? You got to see Julia Roberts?
Are you sure it was her?

HASSAN: I believe so. I ask at end. When she pay.
You Julia Roberts? She laugh. She say 'Yeah, I wish'.
What mean 'I wish'? She Julia Roberts, no?

JASNA: Oh, silly. She was not Julia Roberts, she
looked like her.

HASSAN: I say: I see you in 'Chicago'! Great body
she have.

(he touches Jasna's hips, she jerks away)

JASNA: You have never been in Chicago, why did
you lie?

HASSAN: The film. Chicago.

JASNA: You're thinking of Catherine Zeta-Jones. Julia
Roberts is not in 'Chicago'.

HASSAN: Catherine… I go write poem for Catherine.

JASNA: You can help me with the fucking dinner.

HASSAN: No talk with ffff….! Woman-job dinner. I
am no woman.

JASNA: Gimme a break! You think we're still at
home? Here you can't act as a spoiled prince

anymore. We're nobody here. Get used to that. You are nobody here.

HASSAN: I am no nobody.

JASNA: Okay... How did you spend your week? What did you work on? A new book, a short story, a poem, a haiku, a line? Writing in the mornings, reading in the afternoon?

HASSAN: I do TV.

JASNA: Evenings?

HASSAN: Good program at evening. News. Film. Culture.

JASNA: Try to concentrate on English when you watch a film. Turn the subtitles on.

Alex enters.

ALEX: Hi, mom.

Jasna kisses him, pats his hair. Alex enjoys it first then he jerks away.

HASSAN: Mom got new job. Live with rich Russian. No nights home!

ALEX: No nights home? You don't need to do that, mom! I got a job.

JASNA: Great! What do you have to do?

ALEX: Wash dishes. Exterminate leftovers. I'm Leftover Two. There's this other guy, Leftover One who works with the clean hot water. I work with the dirty hot water. I take orders from a Latino guy, a moron, he can't read or write, talk or think, but he knows everything about fucking explosives, coz he started a revolution in his country, and he knows how to make dirty bombs, you can make a bomb in a fucking bottle, and he's like "you Muslim boy, you know nothing!" and I'm like "Fuck off, what's your problem if I'm Muslim / and he's like...

JASNA: Don't talk like this! What is going on? You've never talked like this. You're not Muslim! Hassan, say something to your son!

HASSAN: No talk like this!

ALEX: Go to the English Kindergarten, pa'!

HASSAN: What he say? What he say?

JASNA (to Alex): You are being rude.

HASSAN: What he say? What Muslim?

JASNA: What's this Muslim thing?

HASSAN: Alex, I am Muslim, you no. And I am no Muslim Muslim, I am American now, you are American, we are American.

ALEX: Good job, dad. You learned how to conjugate the verb to-be-American. They should give you citizenship for that. And a pair of underwear with the American flag imprinted on crotch.

JASNA: Alex!

HASSAN: I do TV. I no talk this boy. I no like this boy.

JASNA: Don't talk like this with him. He's your father!

ALEX (*mockingly*): He's your father!... Mom, you don't have to work there, you don't have to live with the Russians!

JASNA: We need money, Alex.

ALEX: You used to be a hot journalist, now you're nothing, you're shit!

She slaps him. He puts on his jacket.

JASNA: Where are you going? You're not going anywhere! I forbid you to go out. Alex!

ALEX: We live in a free country!

JASNA: Hassan, do something!

Alex exits.

JASNA: Hassan!

HASSAN *(grabbing her by her waist):* He go. OK. We alone… Last night… Tomorrow you go Russians… My bird! Beautiful. You beautiful. Lepa Moja. Ljubavi moja! *(pronounciation: lehpah moyah, lubavi moyah)*

JASNA: Leave me alone…

HASSAN *(touching her):* I am husband. Beautiful wife. Hassan and Jasna. Romeo and Julieta. Long time. Long time…

JASNA: I don't feel like doing it, Hassan.

HASSAN: You beautiful you must. I write poem on you… I play music on you, Jasna … Honeymoon. Belvedere Hotel…The Alps… Honeymoon… *(excited)* Iti amintesti, frumoasa mea, pasarica mea, luna noastra de miere in Alpi? Noi doi in mansarda la hotel, afara inghetat, inauntru fierbinte…

JASNA: I'm sorry, dragul meu, but … *(pushing him away)* I don't want to do it.

HASSAN: You want English? *(stroking her)* Wife duty. Long time. Wife duty, beautiful bird. You bird of honey and dreams. Sky and sand. I take you to stars with limo. Take you to place you never go. Drive to stars, drive to Milky Way, come, little bird, come, kada ste stigli…*(he tries to kiss her)*

JASNA: No, Hassan! I said NO! Nu!

HASSAN: You want English? Here English. Here English! Here English!

(he forces himself on her)

JASNA *(pushing him away)*: Don't turn yourself into animal, Hassan, don't!

Scene 6

We see Vanya and Irina making love in Vanya's bedroom, Irina moans loudly.

Vlady's blog: LONERS' PARTY

VLADY: Abandon Hope and Stupidity, All Ye Who enter this Blog!!!

Imagine that your so-called father is making love in the room next door. No, not with your mother. Your mom is dead. With a young beautiful blonde girl with curly hair and hot tits. Imagine you feel your whole body swelling and shaking. Imagine her legs. Just her legs. Don't try to imagine her lips kissing his lips if you don't wanna puke. You don't wanna puke. You wanna taste. Imagine the place between her legs. A forbidden city. Imagine yourself squeezing inside that city. Walk on those streets. Drink fresh water from those fountains. Stop to contemplate. Tell yourself that's the happiest day of your life. Sightsee. Walk. Run. Look around. Listen to her panting sounds. Music. Hip-hop. Dance. Dance. Faster and faster and faster and faster…

Scene 7

Lights shift to Kebab lying on the sidewalk. He's half covered with a blanket. He wears no shoes, only socks. The moans can still be heard.
Jasna gets out of the house.

Vlady watches them from his window. Jasna lights a cigarette. Kebab jumps us, frightened.

JASNA: It's OK, I just came out to smoke a cigarette. You want one? Here if you want. *(she puts a cigarette on the sidewalk)* You can't sleep either, can you? *(beat)* Those damn moans... *(beat)* It's cold, you should go to a shelter. Did you try to go to a shelter? *(beat)* What's your name?... What is YOUR name?

KEBAB: Name.

JASNA: Good. You can speak. My name is Jasna. Jasna!

KEBAB: Jasna...*(pointing at her)* Alone?

JASNA *(surprised)*: Yes, alone.

KEBAB *(pointing at himself)*: Alone.

They look in each other eyes, a moment of connection.

JASNA: You need shoes, I'm going to bring you some shoes. Do you understand me? You need shoes.

KEBAB: No shoes!

JASNA: Yes, you need shoes. You have big feet... In my country it's a saying: "one lives on big feet". It means one's very rich. Isn't that ironic?... Vlady – you know Vlady? The young man who lives in this house? He calls you Kebab. A nickname. Kebab... If you tell me your name, I can tell him not to call you Kebab anymore. What's your name, Kebab? Name! .... *(she touches his head)* Knock, knock, is anybody there?

KEBAB: Kebab. ... *(he takes the cigarette, Jasna lights it)*

They sit next to each other smoking, in silence.

Scene 8

Lights up on VANYA and IRINA in Vanya's bedroom, in the bed.

They just made love.

IRINA: Yeah, that was good! Fucking perfect... We could do that every night!...

VANYA: It's easy when you're 21.

IRINA: C'mon, don't play ol' daddy with me!

VANYA: I'll see your REAL daddy, ol' comrade Boris, tomorrow in Leningrad.

IRINA: St Petersburg. You're not going to tell him about us, are you? Unless... you're asking for my hand in marriage!

VANYA (slapping her bottom): I'll ask him for your ass
…Don't be silly! You're my waitress, we're not
supposed to fuck our employees, are we?

IRINA: Bull. You all do it or wanna do it. You think
I'm blind or something. Even the most constipated
ones, the ones saying 'my wife and my kids' every
two minutes, all of them wanna do it. There's just a
small "philosophical" difference between those who
are thinking it and those who are doing it…

(she starts kissing him, but hears noises from Vlady's
room) Why can't she put him to sleep, that new
woman you hired… why isn't he sleeping?!…
depression should make you sleepy, antidepressants
are supposed to lower your energy, aren't they? How
can someone who can't move make so much noise?

VANYA: Who's talking about making noise…

IRINA: And that woman, the Albanian or Romanian,
whatever, Macedonian, why can't she do something!
You pay her to do something! I'm going to wake her
up. Does she understand any English, does she? I'm
going/ to…

VANYA *(pulling her back):* Stop acting like a spoiled brat. Or I and daddy Boris will have a very unpleasant conversation …

IRINA: You're blackmailing me?!… You … Gangster! *(Vlady makes more noise)* That woman is good for nothing, / I saw her, she's….

VANYA: Listen, girl. You leave Jasna alone!

IRINA: Oh, my God, you like her, you wanna fuck her! You wanna try an older chick, a married woman, a new thrill, I can see that, / I see…

VANYA: Look, Irinka, this doesn't work. We had fun, but you're young, you're beautiful, you should find someone your own / age to be with… *(he gets out of bed)*

IRINA: No way! Don't you start telling me you're young, you'll find someone else, this is so… corny, it can't happen to me, no way, not now, when you're leaving tomorrow and… not now, when I'm, when I'm fucking in love with you, you fucking gangster!

VANYA: Shhhhhhhh. This business trip to Leningrad is crucial, Irina. I'm sorting things out. When I get back I'm gonna open a new restaurant on Wall Street, a hotel in Brighton Beach, one in Florida, and a TV station for the East European community. I'm going to hire you to do PR. I go public. I go big.

IRINA: You think I'm stupid, you think I don't know what business you're into, you think I can't see you swimming in that Big Oil Business, B.O.B., let's call it B.O.B, you think I don't hear you talking on your cell phone in Japanese and Arabic, you think I don't understand Japanese and Arabic? You're right, I don't, but I get the sense, I'm Russian-Italian from Vegas, I know you're sunk in that oil shit up to your mouth, you're full of shit, you, daddy, that Japanese guy, that Israeli Mafioso, that Ukrainean Tarzan, everybody, all the guys you're doing business with, crooks, gangsters, Organizatsyia, KGB Mafia…

VANYA: Watch your mouth, girl!

IRINA: Or what, or what? You're gonna kill me, have someone cut me into pieces, shove them in a plastic bag, put it in a suitcase and ship it over… where? Caribbean maybe? You promised me a trip to the

Caribbean. And stupid me I thought I'd get there alive!

VANYA: Shhhhhhh. We're getting out of here, I drive you home. *(he starts dressing)*

IRINA: We're not getting out, oh no, I'm telling you, you're not out like this, this is not that easy, this is not a call you make, "I'm out", you're not out, you can't be out, it's too late to be out, you're in, you're fucking in, I'm fucking... *(silently)* pregnant.

VANYA: With me?... Don't you have a boyfriend, don't you sleep with guys your own age, your colleagues, a student, somebody... It can't be me...

IRINA: What? *(pause)* It's you...

VANYA: OK. You say you're pregnant. That's fine. I mean it's not fine, but it's not an unsolvable problem. We can take care of this. We don't want to create problems for anyone, do we? Let's see. Do you want a nice car, what kind of car does my pretty little girl want, my sunshine, my sweetheart? Do you want a Porsche?

IRINA: I wanna a Porshe… to run over your dick with!

Scene 9

In front of the house.

JASNA *(Kebab gestures he wants another cigarette):* Sure. Let's smoke all of them tonight!

KEBAB: Smoke. *(he takes a bunch of cigarettes)*

JASNA: It's OK, Kebab. I really needed to be with a stranger tonight. With a complete stranger… Do you know that feeling - to want to erase all your memories, every single inscription in your brain and on your body, and start fresh, make a fresh start?

KEBAB: Start!

JASNA: Thank you, Kebab. I'll try to follow your advice.

Vlady opens the window.

VLADY*(shouting at Jasna)*: I jump in five!

One…Two…

JASNA: Go ahead, Vlady, life is miserable, isn't it?

VLADY: Three…

JASNA: The problem is you won't die jumping from the second floor. If you need a painful broken arm, it's gonna work. Go ahead, jump!

VLADY: Four!

JASNA: Can you wait until I finish my cigarette, please?

Vlady slams the window and goes away from it.

Jasna sighs with relief, she was actually very tensed but managed to hide it well.

Vanya storms out of the house.

VANYA: He locked himself in his room! Who gave him the key? *(he notices the window still open)* Did he try to jump out the window? I'm gonna put bars at that window!

JASNA: It's OK. He was just joking. There's no need for bars.

VANYA: Did you give him the key?

JASNA: I left it in the door. I didn't know I was supposed to keep it.

VANYA *(coldly)*: You are supposed to keep it all the time.

Scene 10

Vlady's blog: LONERS' PARTY

VLADY: Not all women are pussies. There are women who are not afraid of Death. There are women who can smoke calmly their cigarette and stand under a rain of bombs. Women who can make love when everything around them is in flames. Bombs and orgasms. Big deaths, little deaths. The universe delivers His last monologue for her and she fucks the universe...

I could love this woman, but she's too old, she could be my mom. Her name is Jasna.

Lights on Alex in an internet cafe.

ALEX: Mom, check your damn email, mom, check it! It must be nice living in that rich posh house, taking care of that spoiled Russian brat... You totally forgot about us. Dad cried in his soup today. I am the one who cooked, I made soup for both of us. Chicken soup. He doesn't do anything. He just sits in front of the TV, turned on mute, and declaims poems in Bosnian and Romanian. It's crazy in this house, mom.

At school it's bad but at home it's even worse. I feel like making a bomb and blowing up all this shit! fucking YOURS,

Alex

Scene 11

Lights shift to Jasna in the living room. 3 pm. Jasna dusts furniture. Vanya enters carrying his travel bag.

VANYA: Did the cab arrive?

JASNA*(looks out the window)*: I don't see any cab.

VANYA: What's Vlady doing?

JASNA: Playing games. On the computer.

VANYA: Please be very careful with him. He is quite inventive when it comes to suicide.

JASNA: Did you say "good bye" to him?

VANYA *(beat, flirtatious)*: You should dye your hair red, Jasna. Your eyes will shine under red / hair…

JASNA: You should say "good bye" to Vlady.

VANYA: You know what I see when I look at you: a pretty turtle hiding her body inside a shell of bad memories.

JASNA: When I look at you I see those framed photos I dusted in your bedroom. The old comrades in white suits "with bellies", your pals it seems…

VANYA: Oh please, don't include me in the "old comrades with white bellies" category.

I would hate to fire a woman like you. With such a fire in those Mary Poppins eyes…

JASNA: I would hate to have to quit on such short notice.

VANYA: Why, didn't you like my pun: fire-fire? I think it's a good one. (*she turns to leave*) OK, OK, let's stop this hot Cold War. I get the message.

JASNA: You have a girlfriend who could be my daughter!

VANYA: Or my granddaughter…

JASNA: I should go to Vlady's room. I don't want to let him play DOOM too long.

VANYA: He gets totally crazy each time I go to Russia. Last year he cut his wrists and wrote "Fuck Lenin!" and "Murda!" in blood, on the wall…

JASNA: I think I can handle him.

VANYA: What's your secret, what 'superkalifragilistik' spell you know, jasna-Jasna?

JASNA: My great grandma' was a Gypsy so... I might know a few spells!

VANYA: No kidding? Gypsy blood too... You scare me! How much do you charge for a good-spell session?

JASNA: You need one for the trip?

VANYA: Look: I don't want any guests in my house, Jasna. Even if someone calls and tells you he is my friend, even if he stops you on the street and you recognize him from those photos in my bedroom, yes, especially if he is in those photos, don't let him enter my house, don't let him talk to Vlady!

JASNA: So things are not going very well in the red kingdom of white bellies...

VANYA: Can I trust you in this matter, Jasna?

JASNA: OK. No white-suit-with-belly in this house, I can promise that. Anything else?

VANYA: Dye your hair! Make it bright red.

JASNA (*pretending she didn't hear that, looking out the window*): The cab is here.

In his room, Vlady starts making noise.

VANYA: Tell him I said "good bye".

Vanya leaves.

Scene 12

Lights up on Vlady's room. He plays DOOM with the volume turned very loud. Jasna enters.

VLADY: Aaaah, I've been hit by a bomb! I think it was a Serbian or a Croatian.

JASNA: This is not funny!

VLADY: I'm dead! (*pretending he's dead*) Dead.

JASNA: Vlad, stop this!

VLADY: What? Wasn't your house hit by a mortar bomb or something?

JASNA: I'm not gonna talk about that with you.

VLADY: Why not? I'm a corpse. Smell me! I know that corpses turn you on, c'mon baby! Come and stick your finger into this wound, / yeah baby! That's great, feel the blood!

JASNA (*trying to ignore him*): OK. Let's see what we're doing today. Something practical. Let' see. OK. Today we get rid of all these shoes. They are old and full of dust, you don't need then anymore, we keep only those who fit you.

(*she starts gathering the shoes*)

VLADY: We can't do this, man! The Motherfucker will be mad.

JASNA: What has Vanya got to do with these shoes?

VLADY(*getting nervous*): They're from him, man. All these shoes are his presents for me in the past 10 years, man. They're Russian shoes. See? He brings them from over there. A new pair every few months. It's kinda funny coz he knows I can't walk with them, but still… It's nice to have shoes, I like to have shoes, man, lots of shoes, they're my army… (*rapping*)

They're my ticket to freedom

They're my ticket to jail

Touch my shoe, nigga

And you go to hell!

JASNA: Jesus. You guys have a weird shoe-thing going on... You say you hate him but you love the shoes from him. This tells me something: deep, inside you, you love your father, you should be able to come to terms with this love. To let it flourish. It will make you feel better.

VLADY: Click! Let's change the "channel", sista. I hate them soap-operas, yo.

He goes back to playing Doom.

VLADY: Booooom! Bazoooom! Baaang!

JASNA: You know what, Vlad: Get a life, start living! Instead of self-pity and stupid suicide attempts, you better get real, take control of your life, prove to your dad that you're strong, that you don't need a nurse! Kill that fucking past of yours, Vlad, bomb your bad memories, murder your fears, murder what holds you back and keeps you from fucking starting your life! Take my advice, Vlady, get real!

Scene 13

Vlady's blog: LONERS' PARTY

VLADY: Get real. Get a life. Words. Words. Words. Kill your past. How the fuck can you kill your past? Can you just delete it? Delete. Delete. You have to delete your childhood first. Then you have to erase your birth. How can you erase your birth without killing yourself? Question mark. Thinking. Thinking. Thinking. Revelation: There's only one way. You have to be up for something big. Really big. Smiley face.

Scene 14

Lights shift to the living-room. Christmas' Eve.

A small white undecorated Christmas tree. Julie Andrews singing carols.

Jasna sets up the table trying to look cheerful.

Vlady and Irina sit at the table without looking at each other.

JASNA: It's a good day. *(beat)* A good day. *(beat)*

VLADY: yeah sista… a day to wonderin' like.. "What the fuck did I do?"

Niggas like you probably snitch.. do a nigga then get rich!

Niggas like you always fit.. 6 feet deep inside a ditch murda / murda murda...rule!

JASNA: Vlady, please... not today! It's Christmas' Eve.

The bell rings. They all look at each other. The bell rings again. They don't move. A small explosion – like loud firecrackers - can be heard. Jasna runs to the window. He sees Alex downstairs, shouting. She runs downstairs and out of the house.

ALEX: Mom! Jasna! Here's a small "cocktail Molotov" in your honor, cheers! Firecrackers! Mom! Dad went to bed at fucking 6 pm! There are no more clean socks in the drawer, mom! Once upon a time I had a ma' and a grandma' who'd nag me: no day without changing your socks! Where are my clean socks, mom? I wear dirty ones, / I feel like shit when someone looks down at me feet, what if they smell and I can't feel the smell, because I got used with the smell, I'm getting used with the dirty me while my mom lives in a clean posh house!

JASNA *(could overlap Alex's or not):* Why are you doing this, Alex, why are you doing this? It's dangerous, it's crazy! You'll get us deported! Shhhh! I don't want to hear a word from you. Try to behave, try to be nice – you are a nice kid, Alex, I know you, you are my son! Shhhh!

Now try to make some friends here, for God's sake! And leave me alone!

VLADY: Yo, painful!

IRINA: Crazy…

VLADY: Cool crazy.

Jasna brings Alex in the living room.

JASNA: This is Alex. Vlady. Irina.

VLADY: Niggas like you always fit.. 6 feet deep inside a ditch

murda / murda murda…rule!

JASNA: Vlad, please! *(to Alex)* What? Why are you looking at me like this?

ALEX: He's just quoting Ja Rule. *(to Vlady)* Ja Rule is not hot any more, dude. It's cold soup.

VLADY: You know nothing, sucker!

JASNA: No arguments today. Truce! Sit down, Alex, you provoked enough excitement today! Everybody's trying to behave now. That's the deal we have. OK?... We are trying to induce that old pleasant domestic Christmas spirit. The smell of cookies, the red socks, the tree. The smiles. The friendship. Everything will be perfect today.

Alex sits at the table.

IRINA: It's very nice of you, Jasna, but, you know, this whole Christmas thing is kinda corny, kinda cliché...

JASNA: You don't like it, you're free to go dear. That's it. Today we're trying to be corny, not horny...

VLADY: Ay, on the spot!

JASNA: And... tah-dah-dam... old-fashioned Jasna has cooked!

ALEX: Do you really need to act like a clown, mom?

JASNA: I'm trying to act like a mom, Alex.

VLADY: Gimme the food, man

gimme ma meal

I ain't in the mood

to be cut to be real

where's the deal

man, where's ma food

Dig it, yo! I'm good.

ALEX: That's not Ja Rule...

VLADY: That's me, fag. Stuff pops out of my brain

too...

ALEX: Stupid stuff, dick.

JASNA: Alex, please! *(the kids sit in silence)* OK. I'm

going downstairs to give Kebab his Christmas dinner.

IRINA: The guy is Muslim, Jasna. He doesn't care

about Christmas. Vanya tried to get rid of him a few

times, but he keeps coming back. Coz Misha gives

him food from the restaurant.

JASNA: Good for him! I wish you guys think a bit of

Kebab living there in the dumpster before talking like

spoiled brats...

ALEX: Yeah, mom, give us the moralistic speech.

IRINA: Plus, we have this ugly naked plastic Christmas tree. You could have told me to bring some decorations. I could have bought a real tree.

VLADY: I like white plastic trees. Whadda fuck's your problem, bitch?! You invited yourself here, to my home, yo, you're a pain in my ass.

IRINA: It's Vanya's home and Vanya is my boyfriend.

VLADY: Nigga, don't make me laugh!

JASNA: Hello! Peace. OK? Peace. You may decorate the Christmas tree with… lettuces, shoes, laces, pills, grenades, whatever … just light little carrots in it! I don't care. Whatever it takes to be… non-cliché!
I want to see you talking nicely to each other when I come back!

(she takes a bottle of vodka out of a red sock)

Tah-nah-naaam! A bottle of Stolichnaya for all of you, with greetings from Santa. It melts the anger. It warms the hearts…

ALEX: We're not 21, mom, we're not supposed to drink alcohol.

IRINA: I'm 21!

VLADY: You're not a nerd, man, are you?

JASNA *(winking)*: It's Vodka for kids...

She leaves. Long pause.

VLADY: Cock and pop again, baby…

men will be men

I spit off 10… fuck it, give 'em the 16

Like my guns dirty and hands clean..

IRINA: Can't you talk like people?

ALEX: It's Ja Rule again. "Fuck you".

IRINA: Did you say fuck you to me, boy?

VLADY: It's the name of the piece, woman.

IRINA: Don't fucking 'woman' me, OK?

VLADY: You're his woman, what the fuck are you doing here, bitch? He's in Russia. Go after him. Fuck him to death, man. Murda!

ALEX: Don't talk to a lady like this, dude.

VLADY: Where's the lady, nigga? And you know what. You don't tell me how to spit in my own glass, fucker…

ALEX: She's not your spittoon, weirdo…

IRINA: Hey. Calm down, boys. *(to Alex)* Ignore him. He's... depressed.

VLADY: Yo, I'm what?

IRINA: You're not feeling well.

VLADY: Bullshit, fuck

I'm at my peak

I'm a freakin' weirdo,

I'm a motherfuckin' freak!

ALEX: Great you admit it.

VLADY: Thanks, man. Gee, you're kinda kind. Kinda girlish. I thought Muslim guys were supposed to be tough.

IRINA: You're Muslim? Why do you celebrate Christmas then?

VLADY: He's only half-Muslim, man. He celebrates it with the other half of his brain.

ALEX: I'm not celebrating Christmas, I came here to see my mom.

IRINA *(drinking)*: Do you Muslims celebrate anything at this time of the year?

VLADY: What religion will your baby have, ho? Given Vanya is an atheist and, you know…

IRINA: What, what baby?

VLADY: Yo, you're crying loudly, woman. I can hear you fucking. I can hear you crying. I ain't deaf, you know... 80% of the fuckin' freakin' mechanism is working.

IRINA: It should be sleeping after 9 pm. Are you allowed to stay awake that late?

ALEX *(to IRINA)*: Are you gonna be Vlad's step-mother?

VLADY: Uuuuh, mommy! You're hot, mommy! Gimme a lit'l bro, mommy!

IRINA: This… smart-ass. He loves to show off. To freak us out. "Yo, man *(She stands up, goes to Vlady and starts doing a sort of mockery lap-dance.)* I'm all fucked up so I love when y'all are fucked-up /… but still, I'm the most fucked up and I'm enjoying this… Murda murda murda murda….

VLADY *(without touching her):* Go on, woman. Give it to me! Give it to me! Now you're talking sense. I like that. You're talking sense! Yeah, baby, you're talking sense.

Murda me... murda me... yo ... Yeah!

ALEX: You're both nuts.

IRINA *(going back to her place):* I am nuts to be spending Christmas with high school kids...

ALEX: I'm not in high-school.

IRINA *(drinking)*: Sure...

VLADY: Don't bullshit the "lady", man...

ALEX: I quit, dude. School is a brainwashing institution, man. They teach you not to think with your own mind. To obey stupid rules. To conform to stupid teenage stereotypes. They give you some shit: parties, cheer chicks, pot... to keep you dreamy and stupid, you know... to turn your mind away from the real stuff.

VLADY *(drinking)*: I hear you, brother...

IRINA: That was so bold of you, Alex! To quit. Yeah! I'm with you. I was a cheer leader and I quit. It seemed so stupid to bounce around for a victory that wasn't even mine… And your English is so good, how long have you been in America?

ALEX: I managed to scare them fast, didn't I?

VLADY: The big-bad Muslim wolf.

IRINA: Did you do anything like… bad, or you just quit?

ALEX *(drinking)*: They gave us this stupid essay assignment. Something political, blah, blah. But also poetic. Blah-blah… I wrote about the last minutes of a woman suicide-bomber. I talked about the cold explosives glued to her hot tits. I described in details her fuse-like nipples and combustible belly. The fire inside of her and outside of her. The explosion. The pieces of her flesh flying like decapitated birds… It scared the shit out of them. I got detention for three days. I escaped after three hours.

IRINA: Wow. You're something. *(drinking)* Cheers!

VLADY *(drinking)*: Cheers, bro!

ALEX *(drinking):* Cheers!

IRINA *(to Alex)*: You're awesome. Fearless. And I like your language. "Combustible belly". "Fuse-like nipples". Cool. You're really talented, you're a poet.

ALEX: Well, I never wrote a real poem ...

VLADY: Listen to the babe, man, you're a poet!

IRINA: Tell me, Alex, did you ever consider.... you know, blowing yourself up?

ALEX: It passed through my mind, yeah.

IRINA: Yeah?!

ALEX *(looking for the right words)*: Yeah, but, I kinda like... life, you know, life can be shitty but, you know, it's still life, I mean here in America, it's not so bad after all, there are places where life is really shit, but not here, here is kinda cool, I mean if you don't really put up with all the shit they teach you, / it's kinda...

IRINA: You're so right! And so well put.

VLADY: Hey guys, yo, are you up for something big? I mean really BIG.

IRINA: What do you mean BIG?

VLADY: Murda!

IRINA: You're crazy.

VLADY: I'm serious. I'm real. We put a bomb under his table. Booooooom! His dick goes pop, fireworks… Whadda ya say, are you in?

IRINA *(drinking)*: Who are you talking about?

VLADY: Vanya, who else. The motherfucker.

IRINA *(laughing hysterically)*: The shit deserves a real blow-job. Yeah! I'm in! Great idea, Vlady!

VLADY: Hey. I'm serious here. I'm freakin' serious! I'm damn fuckin' serious!

ALEX: I hear you, dude. I hear you.

IRINA: OK. We're serious.

ALEX: Why do we want the guy out?

IRINA: He's a gangster. Did you hear of Organizatsya? Russian Mafia? He's in! I'm positive, he's in.

ALEX: How can you be so sure?

VLADY: The woman fucks him, holmes, c'mon, she knows.

IRINA: I heard him talking on the phone with ``Tarzan'' Fainberg . You know, Porky's owner. You watch the News? The guy in Florida who got convicted for racketeering and smuggling a few years ago. Last week he called Vanya from jail!

VLADY (drinking): Boo!

IRINA: He blackmails people. He has secret information about them. I heard him three times saying: Do you want them to know you worked for us?

ALEX: Got it. The guy's a shark. We want the shark to, say, retire?

IRINA: That's the word. He must retire!

ALEX (to Vlady): Are you sure about this? He's your... father.

VLADY: He killed my mom.

ALEX (drinking): Oh, shit!

IRINA: He did that?

VLADY (drinking): Bought her a car, man. A Porsche. Did somethin' to it. Next day she was dead. Yo, murda!

IRINA: He wanted to buy me a Porsche too...

VLADY (whispering): He's KGB!

ALEX: No kidding?! The KGB?

VLADY: The big KGB! And he's a general or something. A big boss. Under cover.

ALEX (*drinking*): That's serious. KGB did some huge shit in my country.

IRINA: I'm gonna kill that freakin' KGB monster!

VLADY: Facts, man, not words, fuckin' facts, sista, not poetry! (*to Alex*) Question. Where do we get the bomb from, brother?

IRINA (*drinking*): You have a source, Alex, don't you?

VLADY: Don't you?

ALEX: I can get some explosives.

VLADY: You're not a chicken, man. Yo! Cheers, comrades! Down to the bottom!

IRINA/ALEX: Down to the bottom!

They drink their glass of vodka in one gulp.

VLADY: Let's talk talks now. When can we have the 'fireworks', yo, Muslim bro?

ALEX: When is he coming back?

IRINA: He must be back for the New Year's Eve. He's got to host the party in the restaurant.

VLADY: Then we need to have the "thing" asap. When he shows up, we need to be fast, man, to take him by surprise. He's not stupid, yo.

IRINA (*drinking, tipsy*): He's devilish. He invited three women to accompany him to the party, can you believe that, three!? All under 25.

VLADY: Women! You have two days, Alex. Can you manage, bro?

ALEX: I might need more / than two days…

VLADY: C'mon! Don't be a pussy now. We need to start the New Year fresh.

IRINA: C'mon, Alex, let's see some fireworks!

ALEX (*drinking*): OK. Deal.

VLADY: All right, sista, you can plant it down there in the back room, underneath his table, can't you?

IRINA: Sure. But… it won't destroy the whole restaurant, will it?

ALEX: Only a few meters around.

IRINA: I mean… the customers shouldn't be in danger.

ALEX: It's gonna be just for him.

IRINA: Are you sure you can control the explosion?

VLADY: Of course he can. He's a pro.

ALEX: I think I can.

IRINA: He's not sure.

ALEX: I'm sure!

VLADY: Hey, dude. I live up here, I take the big risk. But I trust Alex.

ALEX: It's gonna be OK. Just a little tiny mess.

VLADY: We're good then. Yo, deal?

(beat)

VLADY: Deal, brothers?!

ALEX: Deal.

IRINA: Deal!

VLADY *(drinking)*: Well done, comrades!

ALEX: You've got any cash for this? We gonna need some cash.

VLADY: Yep. I've got some savings. We're all banked, man.

ALEX: OK. We're good then.

VLADY: We must close this deal in blood.

He takes a knife from the table.

IRINA: Oh, no!

VLADY: Are you afraid, little girl?

IRINA: I'm not, but… *(drinking)* I hate to see blood.

VLADY: Then maybe you're not up for the task. Yo?

ALEX *(taking another knife)*: You don't need to cut very deep. Here… on your finger!

He cuts himself.

VLADY: You're the man, man! *(he cuts himself on the palm)* Here. On my life line!

IRINA: Ew. *(to Alex)* Can you cut for me?

VLADY: You gotta do it yourself, man. And hurry, I'm getting all dirty with blood and shit...

IRINA *(cutting her finger)*: OK. Done. Ew.

VLADY: Gimme your hands, man! *(they join their cut hands)* Yo! Let our blood be the ink on the contract, let our hands be the paper on which we all sign, today, we all swear today, we, Alex – the Muslim, Irina – the former cheer leader, and Vladimir - the Russian Brain, we are ready to go as far as it takes to give some meaning to this brainwashing life, to kill a piece of Evil as our small good deed for this world, where people should be comrades, but they're not, yo, let the blood witness our bond through silence and MURDA!

ALL: MURDA!

END ACT I

ACT II

Scene 15

Vlady's blog: LONERS' PARTY

VLADY: Why does she come upstairs when he's not here? She sneaks up in there, in his bathroom, and: CRIES… Creepy!… And the funny thing, man, is a funny thing, man… I like to listen to her crying. It's kinda… refreshing. Lullaby, man. She's crying in low tone, like in her hands, low volume, no loud squeaks like when they fuck… Sometimes she lets the water pour in the bathtub, she dives in, man, it's like I can almost fuckin' see her… I never gave a shit about crying. I never thought it was musical or other shit like this, but it is, hers is… yo, glad we've got two freakin' bathrooms, man, I don't wanna see her crying when I gotta take a piss!

Lights up on Alex in an Internet Cafe.

ALEX: Hey, dude, Vlad. I'm still working on the THING. It's weird, you know, this feeling: the power of life and death. It's like making love with a platoon of angels until your body explodes into a cosmic orgasm. *(beat)* Send.

Lights up on Irina writing on a laptop.

IRINA: Check your email, Vanya, check your fucking email!... I'm doing it, I'm doing it. I'm getting rid of it. You don't want it, I don't want it, who the fuck wants it? Why to bring someone into this world – this world sucks! I've made up my mind. I don't want to give Life to anything. I want to give Death. D.E.A.T.H. Death. Death. *(beat)* Send.

She starts crying.

Jasna enters Vanya's bedroom.

JASNA: Irina… *(beat)* Irinushka… This is not good. There is no point in crying. You cannot cry for a man unless he died or got killed. There is nothing to get from crying. Men hate women who cry. You know that. You must know that. Men like us only when we are powerful, confident, beautiful. They are very insecure, Irinka.... They need us to be strong. I know that all these sound so cliché, and they actually are clichés, but what are clichés other than old well-proven truths?

C'mon, Irina! Get up, wash your face, put on a smile and go out and flirt!

Scene 16

Lights shift to the sidewalk.

Kebab decorates a little bush with trash cans and other garbage items.

Jasna gets out of the house and walks to him. She caries a plastic bag.

KEBAB: Tree!

JASNA: Wow! A garbage Christmas tree ... But Christmas was five days ago, Kebab...

KEBAB: You like?

JASNA: Yes, it's wonderful…

KEBAB: Tree.

JASNA: I brought you some lunch, food.

KEBAB: Lunch.

JASNA: Yesterday we had polenta, today is soup. You like chicken noodles soup, don't you?*(she gives him the soup, he starts eating, she lights a cigarette)* What a beautiful sad face you have, Kebab... What are you actually doing here? America is for smiley faces, for active people with clear goals... When I was a journalist I used to write about people like you. I would dig into their souls, throw question after question, until I found it: the locked room where the dark secrets lie. The hidden dirt under the carpet. The shameful photos under the bed. The pain lingering under their skin...What's your secret, Kebab?

KEBAB: Lunch. Good.

JASNA: I'm glad you like it.

She smokes, he eats, in silence.

JASNA: Speaking about goals, guess what I have for you? *(she takes a pair of shoes out of her bag)* Tah-dah-dam: Shoes!

KEBAB: No shoes!

JASNA: I stole them for you. Vlady has too many...

KEBAB (*agitated all of a sudden*): No shoes! Kebab bad,
Jasna, Kebab bad!

JASNA: No, you're not bad!

KEBAB: Go, go! Go shoes, no shoes! (*he throws away
the shoes*)

JASNA: Calm down, Kebab!

KEBAB: Plane. Sky. Bad. Kebab bad…

JASNA: What plane?

KEBAB: Sky, bomb, shoe-bomb…

JASNA: A shoe-bomb?!

KEBAB (*gesturing*): Woman sit here…

JASNA: On the plane…

KEBAB: Old woman… grandmother… America

JASNA: On the plane to America, an old woman?

KEBAB: She smile … "want place at window, son,
look at sky?"…. Yes, I say yes, sky, blue sky…

JASNA: You are on the plane to America, sitting next
to an old woman….

KEBAB: Yes, plane…Change seat… Look sky… I
cannot do now, I cannot… Sky upside-down,
beautiful, blue sky… I cannot… I smile… I smile like

woman … Mission I cannot now, I cannot shoe-bomb… I cannot do… later… later… but I cannot, I cannot…

JASNA: Oh, my God…

KEBAB: Bomb explode in Kebab. In heart. I bad, Jasna, / I bad!

JASNA: It's OK, Kebab. You did a good thing. You didn't do it. You're not bad. It's OK. It's OK… *(he buries his head in her lap)* I'm your friend. Jasna is your friend.

Scene 17

VLADY *(writing on the laptop):* Tears… Drowning in a sea of tears…

Irina enters, she stops in the door.

IRINA: Hey.

VLADY: Hey.

IRINA: Can I come in?

VLADY: Yeah. Sure.

Pause. She's inspecting the room. Vlady grows increasingly nervous.

IRINA: So... this is your famous room. The famous shoes. Yeah. You really keep them in order.... You know... Your room is pretty cool. Mine is a total mess, you don't wanna see it. It's gross. I hate it. I totally hate it. It's like a rats' cage... Oh, you got a nice view here! I mean - the street. People. I like to watch people.

VLADY: Yeah... Me too.

IRINA: I mean, you know, my dad's rich, and I still get only $1200 a month. I have to work as a waitress. Just because dad thinks that I must face the "real life". Fuck "the real life"! Real life sucks.

VLADY: Yeah.

IRINA: You used to be more talkative, didn't you?

VLADY: Right.

IRINA: Did I interrupt anything?

VLADY (beat): You cried a lot yesterday. And the day before yesterday. I kinda expected that flood of tears to get over here too...

IRINA: Oh. You heard me. Sorry.

VLADY: It's OK.

IRINA: I won't cry anymore. It's over.

VLADY: You're over him? *(beat)* You're too pretty for him.

IRINA *(flirtatiously)*: You think I'm pretty?

VLADY: Yeah... very.

IRINA: So... he's gonna be dead meat soon...

VLADY: Yep.

IRINA: He's coming back tomorrow. I told you he wouldn't miss the New Year's Party. There's gonna be like 120 people in the restaurant.

VLADY: He called you…

IRINA: He was kinda sweet on the phone.

VLADY: Yo, and you're already all wet, or what? The flood just moved two stairs down, under your belly. Those little tears are all gone, and there she is, the little hot'n'throbbing pussy, waiting for Mister Dick Dickovich!

IRINA: Don't talk like this to me! I'm game. I'm gonna do the "thing".

VLADY: Yeah?!

IRINA: Yeah.

VLADY: You still want him, I can see that, you fucking want him!

IRINA: You can't see anything.

VLADY: You stupid bitch, fucking / stupid... bitch!

IRINA: Careful!

She kisses Vlady on his lips. Then she bites him. Vlady's in pain.

IRINA: Bitches bite.

Scene 18

Vlady's blog: LONERS' PARTY

VLADY: Abandon Hope and Stupidity, All Ye Who enter this Blog!!!

Bite. Bite. Bite. Bite. Bite. Bite. Bite. Bite. Bite. Bite. Bite. Bite. Bite. Bite. Bite. Learn to bite.

Scene 19

Lights shift. Jasna sits on a bench next to Kebab.
It's a beautiful winter day. She holds a book in her lap.
Kebab looks up at the sky. He wears shoes.

JASNA: Don't forget our goal: you must learn English. You're a smart man, you learn quickly. Why do you need to learn English? To be able to start a new life, get a job, normal things that normal people do. This is the story that matters: Kebab's rehabilitation and reinvention.

KEBAB: Re- ?

JASNA: See, that's why you need to learn English. *(back to the book)* Say "this is my car".

KEBAB: This is my car.

JASNA: What color is your car?

KEBAB: My car is red.

JASNA: Great! Whose car is red?

KEBAB: I don't have a car…

JASNA: I know. But we learn new words now and we must put them in sentences, so you can learn how to use them… Let's see… Question. Is your car blue?

KEBAB: The sea is blue.

JASNA: Wonderful! But try to answer the question: Is your car blue?

KEBAB: The sky is blue.

JASNA: Right. But what about the car?

KEBAB: A plane is on the blue sky.

JASNA: OK. Let's try something else. What color is your shoe?

KEBAB: A brown shoe on the blue sky.

JASNA: Yes, it's a brown shoe. But let's forget about the sky for a moment. Let's get more grounded, OK? How many shoes do you have? Two. Say two.

KEBAB: Two shoes on the blue sky.

JASNA: OK. If you love so much the damn sky, let's use it. Count how many shoes are on the sky, count to ten! One shoe…

KEBAB: Ten brown shoes on the blue sky.

JASNA: Kebab, you're not doing what I'm telling you to do.

KEBAB: I am a brown shoe on the sky. Dead.

JASNA: Hey. I didn't teach you this! You're not dead. Dead means… you cannot breathe, you cannot walk, you cannot talk. Can you understand this? You are not dead!

KEBAB: The sky is dead. The / sky is _

JASNA: Alive! You are alive! We are alive.

KEBAB: Alive?

Scene 20

Vlady's bedroom. The backpack with the bomb is in the middle of the room.

A bottle of vodka is passed among Vlady, Alex and Irina.

They all try to look cool, like there's no big deal to have a bomb there.

VLADY: So, comrades, we're all ready for the "fireworks". Cheers!

IRINA: Cheers!

In the bathroom, Jasna is dying her hair.

We can see the bathroom and Vlady's bedroom at the same time.

JASNA *(to the mirror)*: Cheers!

She smiles at herself in the mirror.

ALEX: Cheers!

VLADY: And that's the sweet little bomb. Hi baby!

IRINA: It's bigger than I thought. Can I look at it?

ALEX: I wouldn't do that.

IRINA: I wanna "try it on"…

She "tries it on" and walks around the room like in a fashion show.

VLADY: Breaking Fashion News : the fancy bomb-outfit!

IRINA: The "Medea" poisoned business-suit!

VLADY: The "Anna Karenina" train!

IRINA: It comes in all shapes, colors and sizes!

Irina and Vlady laugh like in a horror movie. Irina kisses Vlady on the lips, he stops laughing. She kisses him again.

ALEX: Hey, guys, I'm here! The invisible man is here!

Vlady kisses Irina, he bites her lips.

IRINA: Wow! That was good, kiddo! Gotta go now. Must prepare for the big "fashion-show"!

VLADY: Cheers! *(he gulps down his glass of vodka)* Let me hold it for a sec!

Vlady takes the backpack and stares at it.

VLADY: It's not heavy… It's gonna work, bro?

In the bathroom, Jasna has finished dying her hair.

JASNA: Ready for a Pulitzer, huh? The homeless shoe-bomber. The ragged shoe-bomber. The failed shoeless shoe-bomber. *(doubting her "headlines")* Is

shoeless a word?

She sits on the edge of the tube, takes a notebook out of her

other pocket and starts writing.

Vlady's bedroom. Irina grabs the backpack. Alex stares at

her with an empty gaze.

IRINA: It's gonna work. Don't worry, kiddo!

She exits. Pause.

ALEX: I feel kinda bad about all this…

VLADY: Yo! What's wrong with you? We talked

something, man. Murda!

ALEX: Yeah, dude. Yeah.

VLADY: Whadda fuck are you scared of? You want

the man in pieces or not?

ALEX: I don't know, dude… I don't even know the

guy…

VLADY: OK, brother, tell me, tell your nigga what's

nagging at you? You don't wanna have a murda

swimming in your mind, am I right, man, am I right?

ALEX: There's lots of shit going on, man… Dad wants

us to go back home…

VLADY: What home, nigga?

ALEX: Fucking Sarajevo…

VLADY: Forget about Sarajevo, man, we've got stuff to do here, murda!

ALEX: I don't know, dude… This is all wrong, man. It's wrong. Mom says he's kinda cool…

VLADY: Women like him, man. He does something to their brains.

ALEX: He did something to your brain.

VLADY: And we're gonna fuck his brain too, man, this is the game!

ALEX: It's not a game, dude. Wake up! We're not playing a game. It's like you live in another world or something. You don't understand shit!

VLADY: Oh, yeah. Sure. Tell me about shit, nigga. I know the history and the geography of shit by heart, man. I live shit. I breathe shit. I dream shit. Look at me, look at these freakin' legs: jellyfish! Shit! What the fuck is YOUR problem, nigga? You made a fucking bomb, so what?

ALEX: Look, man… I couldn't…

VLADY: What are you trying to say, holmes?

ALEX: It wasn't easy to...

VLADY: What?

ALEX: That bomb in the bag...it wasn't...I tried but...I can't let a girl to...there's no bomb.

VLADY: What? What about your email, your "cosmic orgasm"? What the fuck was that? Poetry? Another one of your stupid high school essays?... I knew it, I knew it from the first moment I saw your fucking face! You ain't got the 'look', man, the 'murda look'... Nigga in the game, ready to die!

ALEX: Shut up, man, you ain't got the "look" either... You're a rich brat who just got bored!

VLADY: Watch your mouth, yo! You coward, you jellyfish, you fucking rat, (he tries to hit Alex) you Bosnian cocksucker, I'm gonna have your mom suck my dick, yo!

ALEX (moving around and touching Vlady from time to time): Yeah, why don't you hit me, man, c'mon, c'mon! Hit me! Hit me!

Vlady desperately attempts to stand up and hit Alex. He falls down.

ALEX: Facts, man, not words. Reality! Not fiction.

VLADY: Leave me alone. Get out of here! Out!

ALEX *(taking a small clock attached to some explosives out of his pocket):* Here's your "toy", man. Connect the red wires and in 10 secs it will explode. Cheers!

He places the "thing" in one of the shoes and leaves.

Vlady stares at the shoe.

Jasna storms in, she has a towel wrapped around her hair.

JASNA: What's going on here? Where is Alex? Vlady, are you all right? Are you hurt?

VLADY: Get me my wheelchair!

JASNA: Let me help you!

VLADY: Get me my wheelchair!

Jasna brings the wheelchair next to Vlady so he can climb in.

JASNA: Alex will pay for this.

Scene 21

Vlady's blog: LONERS' PARTY.

VLADY: Abandon Hope and Stupidity, All Ye Who enter this Blog!

Volodea is four. His mother walks him to the kindergarten. The main square. A crowd cheering. The big bronze statue of Lenin is pulled down. Cheers!

The Father of Communism dangling up in the air. His head down. His feet up. Volodea pulls his hand from his mother's. Where are you going, Volodea? He runs to Father Lenin. "Where are you going, Father Lenin?" The crowd freezes. A cracking wail breaks the silence. The first piece of Lenin falls. It's his shoe. Crushing Vlady's legs. Making him a doomed cripple forever... A doomed rich spoiled cripple... DOOMED. RICH. SPOILED. CRIPPLE. DOOMED. RICH. SPOILED. CRIPPLE ... *(he repeats the last words again and again, like a robot)*

Scene 22

Jasna's apartment. Later. Hassan writes a poem in Romanian.

HASSAN: Eu scriu poeme pe trupul tau aprins

Iar pielea ta-mi raspunde vorbind o limba moarta

Cuvintele in ape si dealuri se preschimb

Si-ti desenez iubirea-mi ca pe-o harta…

(translation: I write poems on your hot body, / your skin answers me speaking a dead language/ my words turn into rivers and hills / and I draw my love for you like a map)

Jasna storms in.

JASNA: Where is Alex?

HASSAN: You dye hair…

JASNA: Where is our son?

HASSAN: You no good mother. No good wife.

JASNA: Don't say that.

HASSAN: You there with Russian! Uncle Vanya!

JASNA: I work there! *(taking a hundred of dollars out of her purse)* Here, money, so you can go and buy some food. Buy pizza, make some pastas, don't have Alex cook for you!

HASSAN: I no pizza, I no pastas. We go back. Home.

JASNA: Home where? Our house in Sarajevo doesn't exist anymore. We can't live again with my parents in Romania. My brother and his wife are there and they're expecting a child / and...

HASSAN: This life - no life. Back Sarajevo.

JASNA: We came here for Alex. To give him a chance for a decent life.

HASSAN: Where decent life? Where? The rich, American in big house, decent life. We no decent life. Home better.

JASNA: We had war back home!

HASSAN: No war now! Only war here, in my soul... I hate limo! I hate rich. I want be Hassan Duric. Good poet!

JASNA: You are a good poet. Your books will be translated, the Americans will get to see how good you are.

HASSAN: I am stupid here. And they not understand metaphor. No soul. No imagination. Home you cursed be poet, you cannot change, you born poet, like disease. Here you go college, you are poet! You say I am poet, you are poet!

JASNA: What do you want, a Poetry Police to say who is and who isn't a poet?

HASSAN: You not understand wife. Mergem acasa!

JASNA: I'm not going back, Hassan.

HASSAN: You are journalist, good journalist home. Here you are servant!

JASNA (beat): It's only temporary, until I get the green card, then I will get a job as a journalist.

HASSAN: You cannot do journalist here. They have American do journalist.

JASNA: I can write stories they cannot write, stories about immigrants, they don't know the details, they don't live like us… Actually I just found a great story!

HASSAN: You wait green card here, I go home.

JASNA: Home is here.

HASSAN: This is no home, Jasna. Home is language where you are born.

JASNA: Home is what you call home.

HASSAN: You call home with Russian? Russians are danger. Russian will do bad to you!

JASNA: You don't know what you're talking about.

HASSAN: I take Alex with me!

JASNA: Alex is a grown-up man who will have to make his own decisions. Like we all do.

She leaves.

HASSAN: Jasna!

Scene 24

Outside the house, on the sidewalk, Kebab leans against the dumpster.

He studies the SHOES he got from Jasna. He notices something at their HEELS.

He plays with the HEEL until it partly detaches itself from the shoe.

Jasna passes by him, ready to enter the house.

KEBAB: Jasna!

JASNA: Leave me alone, Kebab.

KEBAB: Jasna is my friend.

JASNA: I am… I just… I'm not in the mood to talk right now.

KEBAB: This house… Danger. Jasna leave. Leave!

JASNA: I just left my husband. It's enough "leaving" for today…

KEBAB: It's… not good, Jasna. I see Vanya / with…

JASNA: It's not good for YOU to stay here. Go get a job, start living. LIVING, not (she gestures) LEAVING.

KEBAB: Come Kebab. With Kebab.

JASNA: To go with you? To sleep together on the sidewalk, or in a dumpster? You ask too much of me, Kebab.

KEBAB: Leave house. This house. Russian danger.

JASNA: You're the second person who tells me that today. And here's the problem: I like the Russian. I like Vanya. I do. What can I do. I love danger.

KEBAB (beat): Then I go?

JASNA: Yes. Go. Good luck, Kebab.

KEBAB: Come with me!

JASNA (laughing): No. But I can give you some cigarettes and (she looks in her pocket) 20 dollars.

KEBAB (*taking the cigarettes and the money*): Come with Kebab.

JASNA: I'll miss you. But… I have your voice. I have your story, I recorded it.

KEBAB: Recorded?

JASNA: I don't want to bring you any trouble. It's actually better if you go. I can mention you in my article and say that one day you disappeared… No, I can't mention you at all. But… thank you. It was a good story. It made me believe in stories again.

He shows her the shoes.

KEBAB: Shoes. Bad shoes.

JASNA: Take them with you. Wear them.

KEBAB: I go. Danger here.

JASNA: Go!

KEBAB: Come with me!

JASNA: Bye, Kebab. Good luck.

He doesn't move. She kisses him on the forehead and gestures "go".

Kebab exists looking back at Jasna from time to time.

Scene 25

Vanya is in the restaurant's back room, checking some business books/bills and drinking vodka. He's distressed. Half bottle of vodka is empty.

VANYA *(to the bottle of vodka)*: OK. I'm not opening the restaurant this year, but next year for sure. Next year. And the hotels in two years. One on Brighton Beach, one in Florida. One called "The Seagull", one called ... "Cherry Orchard"! *(Jasna enters. She wears a hat.)* Cheers! To you, Vanya!

JASNA: To you, Vanya!

VANYA: Hey, Jasna-Jasna!

JASNA: How was your trip?

VANYA: Could have been better. How are things here? *(half-joking)* I heard everyone's alive and well.

JASNA: Alive, yes.

VANYA: And well?

JASNA: No white suit with belly showed up.

VANYA: They're around... They're coming to the party tomorrow...

JASNA: Bad news, huh?

VANYA *(explodes)*: Those fucking Russians! Now they're all clean, can you believe it? Fucking crooks... the word "failure" is not in my vocabulary, Jasna!

JASNA: The wild-capitalism phase. Everybody stealing from the state. Everybody stealing.

VANYA: All those thieves are now "serious" businessmen, owning corporations, hotels, even seaside resorts!

JASNA: Even restaurants in America.

VANYA: You still think I'm one of them.

JASNA: You could be one of them... And I could write your story. Get a Pulitzer for it.

VANYA: You're back in the journalistic mood?

JASNA: If I write a wild story about you, about your past, about this place, your restaurant will be famous. You'll make lots of money.

VANYA *(amused, in a dangerous way)*: You're playing with fire.

JASNA (*flirtatiously, in a dangerous way*): What else can I do. Fire speaks all languages, lives on all continents. I was stupid to think it could be just left behind.

She takes off her hat.

VANYA: Your hair!

JASNA: Bright red.

VANYA: You're beautiful.

A tender ceasefire. They look at each other, smiling.

JASNA: And … where is my necklace?

VANYA: You thought I forgot… (*he takes a small box out of his bag*) Here!

JASNA (*surprised, she opens the box*): It's gorgeous…

VANYA: It's gold.

JASNA: I love it...

VANYA: Let me help you!

He stands behind her and puts the necklace around her neck. He kisses her neck. A long kiss. Jasna's FACE shows surprise but also pleasure. Then the doubting of that pleasure. The journalist in her screaming: hey, what's going on here?

IRINA shows up, with the bomb-backpack on her shoulder.

IRINA: What the fuck! The cheesiest scene ever! The necklace, the kiss... what the fuck is this? A Russian-Bosnian-Romanian soap-opera!? Is this part of your job description, Jasna?

JASNA *(embarrassed)*: I have to go to Vlady's room.

She rushes to the door. She exits without looking back.

Vanya looks at Irina like nothing happened. He sits down at his table and pours himself vodka in a glass.

IRINA: You don't care about me.

VANYA: Go back to work.

IRINA: Back to work? That's all you have to tell me?

VANYA: I don't need a dramatic scene.

Irina takes a seat in a chair at a different table than Vanya's.

IRINA: Right, let's pretend there wasn't any abortion. Let's erase it from our minds. Such a disgusting thought...

VANYA: I'm sorry. Do you feel all right, did everything go well? Was the money enough?

IRINA (*laughing hysterically*): You really thought I was pregnant? I'm not stupid to let myself get pregnant by you, what did you think?

VANYA: Let's stop this game, Irina.

IRINA: Murda! Murda!

VANYA: Calm down. Do you want some vodka?

IRINA: What about this: Vlad and I planned to kill you. To put a bomb under that table, then run together to Jamaica and live there on your money, fucking and laying in the sun all day long. What about that?

He checks immediately under the table.

IRINA: It's here, in my bag.

VANYA: You don't have a bomb in there, sweetie.

IRINA: Wanna bet? Lovers' leap, lovers' bomb. It's kinda romantic, don't you think?

VANYA: How much time do we have before the 'train-to-heaven' leaves the station?

IRINA: It's the train-to-hell for you! What do you think, baby, honey, asshole, you think I bought us tickets to Cancun or something?

VANYA: You want to see me frightened, that's it? I'm sorry, girl, it's been many years since death doesn't frighten me anymore... Are you going to show me the bomb?

IRINA: You did believe me!

VANYA: Of course, I didn't.

IRINA: I threw the bomb in the East River...

VANYA: OK.

IRINA: But it didn't explode, it didn't. I expected to see an artesian well at the very least. I thought I killed the fish. I cried. First out of anger. Then out of panic. Then out of joy. I like fish. You know, I'm a Pisces...I cannot murder the fish. It's like they're my family, can you understand that?

VANYA: Are we talking Horoscope now?

IRINA: You're lucky, you bastard. I didn't have the balls to kill you.

VANYA: You don't have any reason to do that, sweetie...

IRINA: But I killed your daughter... She was quite big, the doctors said.

VANYA: Are we in the fantasyland again? *(beat)* You know what: I am going to call your dad and apologize I cannot have you working here anymore.

IRINA: You're not going to fire me! You know what: this is my last day of working here. After the party, I'm gone, GONE!

VANYA: I will tell your father I'm immensely sorry to have lost the perfect waitress. The waitress who didn't like to wait. Always nervous. Always rushing. Always / shouting...

IRINA: Guess what, "honey": I will tell my daddy the TRUTH. *(heading towards the door)* By the way, your son, Vlady, is a much better kisser!

<u>Scene 26</u>

Jasna's apartment. The kitchen. Hassan is cooking. Alex enters.

HASSAN: Mom was here. Looking you...

ALEX: Whatever.

HASSAN: I made pastas. With meatballs. Chiftele –
like your grandmother.

ALEX: I'm not hungry.

HASSAN: Very good. You like them. Chiftele.

ALEX: I told you I'm not hungry!

HASSAN: You will.

ALEX: What did mom say?

HASSAN: Where is Alex.

ALEX: Anything else?

HASSAN: Back to journalism.

ALEX: She's gonna work as a journalist again?

HASSAN: Or go home. Back Sarajevo… If you want.

ALEX: I don't! I'm not going back, I told you
thousand of times, you step on my nerves with this
fucking question, why don't YOU go back and leave
me fucking alone?

HASSAN: OK. I just check. OK. OK. OK. OK.

He sits on a chair, defeated.

ALEX: Dad…

HASSAN: It's OK.

ALEX: Tata…

HASSAN: It's OK.

ALEX *(whispering)*: I made a bomb.

HASSAN: It's OK.

ALEX: Dad!

HASSAN: Yes?

ALEX: I wrote a poem.

HASSAN: A poem?!

ALEX: Yes.

HASSAN *(excited)*: Read! Read poem!

ALEX: It's a short / one…

HASSAN: What title?

ALEX: Final countdown. It's when you count like three, two, one, zero… Like a bomb, you know…

HASSAN: Good metaphor. Read!

ALEX: I haven't actually written it down. I know it by heart.

HASSAN: Good. Poets write with heart.

ALEX *(truthfully)*: TREI, DOI, UNU, ZERO

Another year is waiting

TO DIE

Counting down its last seconds

SINGUR, ALONE

In the middle of the universe

In the middle of the desert

In the middle of the sea

Another crippled sailor

In another tiny boat

AFLOAT

Begging the sky

For a "HOW", for a "WHO", for a "WHY"

Begging the sand

For a land

THREE, TWO, ONE, ZERO

And?

Hassan looks proudly at Alex and strokes his hair. Alex looks down.

HASSAN: You are my son.

Hassan sets the table. They eat in silence, both immersed in their own thoughts, but a bond between them can be clearly felt.

Scene 27

Vlady's bedroom. Vanya enters.

VANYA: What did you do to Irina, you little macho? What a surprise! To hear that you were impressive, not crazy and suicidal. What's this new boy&girl stuff?

VLADY: Oh, that. Well. She liked it, man. She liked it a lot. We went on and on for like six hours or so. She came 16 times. She said that it was the fuck of her life, like a bomb blowing up all her thoughts, leaving her there, pulsating, in the rhythm of my thoughts, in the rhythm of my thrusts, in MY rhythm!

VANYA: You know I know when people lie, Vlad. That was my job.

VLADY: You don't know shit. I fucked Irina and she loved it!

VANYA: I know when you're lying, Vlad. It was a hot story though....

VLADY: OK. What about this story: it's the last day of your life, what would you do on the last day of your life? Like the last wish, the last moment of truth. I heard people tell the truth on their last day, is that so? You're an expert, tell me, is that true?

VANYA: Why would you want me dead?

VLADY: Why did you want mom dead?

VANYA: I loved your mom.

VLADY: Mom was too smart. She figured out your shit…

VANYA: Masha was happy with me. You were happy with me too. I would come home after hard work, you'd jump / into my arms…

VLADY: Hard work like torturing someone?

VANYA: Just hard work. Like when you hate it but you have to do it because you're a professional. Like when you hate it but you get used to it. Like when you don't hate it anymore, you just do it. For hours and hours and hours. Because you have two mouths to feed at home. Because you have no choice. Because there's no way back…. But I don't expect you to understand that, Volodea, you've never had to do anything you didn't want to. That's what I've been working for. So you don't have to do something you hate...

He offers Vlady the bottle of vodka. Vlady takes it and drinks.

VLADY: Then why do I hate everything around me?

Vanya strokes his hair.

VANYA: Do you remember that story I used to tell you: The Brave Red Rabbit Knight / in the Red Square?

VLADY: In the Red Square....Yeah... you invented it. It used to change every night. *(passing back the bottle of vodka)*

VANYA: Yes, but it was a nice story.

VLADY: One night you said that the brave Rabbit was scared and he cried. I didn't like that.

VANYA: You liked him strong and funny. *(passing back the bottle of vodka)*

VLADY: I liked that one with the Red Rabbit falling in love with the White Fox.

VANYA: And having pink "rabifox" babies...

VLADY: Crazy stories you invented.... cool crazy.

(passing back the bottle of vodka)

VANYA: After I brought you here to America you didn't want to hear stories anymore...

VLADY: You left us there for 3 more years!

VANYA: But I got you here! I took care of everything. Doctors, papers, visas... Got Masha whatever she opened her mouth to ask for. Got her a Porsche. Last model, the one she wanted. But she was not good with gifts... She crashed the car into a wall. She was drunk... Damn Stolichnaya...*(to the bottle)* It's your fault...

VLADY: Wow! Now that's bullshit. Stinky bullshit, yo! Mom used to cry in the bathroom every fucking night. You cheated on her like a thousand times... You used us! Like you use everything, you trade and fuck and torture and blackmail people, that's who you are! And this is the truth, yo, the naked truth! You and your fucking secrets!

Vlady takes the closest shoe and throws it furiously at Vanya.

Then another one, and another one. Vanya is cornered, he tries to protect himself from the shoes that keep hitting him. Vlady wheels to the other side of the room and takes a shoe with a broken HEEL.

VANYA: Volodea! Stop this! Stop it! Stop it when I say! ... OK, I'll make you stop!

Vlady takes out a microfilm from inside the shoe's heel. Vanya is speechless.

Vlady wheels to the other shoes in the room and removes their heels. Microfilms spring out from each of them.

VLADY: What about this, "daddy", what about this? Some great political plots to be revealed to the "stupid" masses. Whaddabout "Sheherezada" plan to get oil from the Caspian Sea. Russians and Americans financed Osama Bin Laden – and they knew about each other! Compromise for the Gas Pipeline through Romania, Bulgaria and Bosnia. War for Oil. Dollars and Rubles – seed money for Terrorism. Red Mafia: How the Russian Mob has invaded America. Head titles for a year!

VANYA *(beat):* Great job, Vladimir.

Pause. They stare at each other, they confront each other, they "recognize" reach other.

VLADY: Yo, this is something! You don't even blink. You're tough, man, you're a tough KGB guy. A Russian brain. A mafioso. Number One on the CIA list of spies. Number One on the freaking KGB list with double agents. You're somebody. You're Number One on the black list of bad parents.

VANYA *(beat)*: I'm impressed.

VLADY: And I am your crippled son. I'm your weak spot. Your Achilles' heel, … dad.

VANYA *(beat)*: You are… you, Vlad.

Jasna enters. She's wearing an apron with two large pockets.

Vanya tries to look in control of the situation.

JASNA: What's going on here?

VANYA: Let's talk later, my dear.

JASNA *(acknowledging the microfilms)*: What are those?

VLADY: KGB fucking microfilms…

*Jasna goes directly to the microfilms, grabs one, studies it,
then picks up another one and another one... She's excited.*

VANYA: Don't get overexcited, Jasna.

JASNA: That's how you managed to get American
citizenship. You sold them KGB secrets... You're
working for both Americans and Russians?

VANYA: I work for myself. And my family. As
simple as that.

JASNA: You still have KGB secrets to pay them for
years and years of comfortable life...

VANYA: You can share that life with me. With us.

JASNA: Are you proposing marriage to me?

VANYA: If that's what "sharing" means to you, yes.

JASNA: Vlady, he brought you all those shoes
because he knew they would never leave this room.
(to Vanya) You supported his agoraphobia. You
nourished his depression!

VLADY: Yo, he was kinda smart though...

Jasna's HANDS are full of microfilms.

JASNA: I can't let this go, Vanya. This is big! This is
THE story!

VANYA: Sure. Take action, Jasna. Why don't you call the Police? Go ahead, call, prepare yourself to answer the first question: your name and social security number, please, ma'am… You are illegal here Jasna. You don't exist here. Oh, sweetheart, you're not pretty when you're frowning like that. You accentuate that deep wrinkle, like a river, in the middle of your forehead. When you're smiling, it glows like a river in the sun. When you're frowning, / it's like…

JASNA: Don't worry. The newspapers won't publish my photo but the documents you stole from the KGB. *She fills her pockets with the microfilms.*

VANYA: You're delusional, Jasna. There's nothing to be published.

JASNA: I won't tell them where I got the microfilms from. I've never revealed my sources. *(her hands and pockets are full with microfilms)* I'm taking them.

VANYA: You can't do that, honey.

Vanya walks to the door and stands in front of it.

JASNA: You think you can stop me?

VANYA: Jasna, Ya tebya liubliu… I love you.

JASNA: Then let me go.

She struggles to get out but he's stronger, he holds her tight like in a tender embrace.

Vlady looks at them with mixed emotions.

VANYA: Let me tell you a little story, my love. You love stories. Back home in Russia I used to have a beautiful Dalmatian dog. Her name was Ciorni Angel. Black Angel. She had such smart little blackberry eyes…One day Ciorni Angel went mad and bit me. I went mad and shot her. I cried the whole night after that, with her little body in my arms. I loved her so much, but I shot her…

JASNA: I'm not your dog, Vanya.

A weird love-hate moment: Vanya kisses Jasna and she doesn't reject him, she's turned on by his power as her past takes over her again. They are immersed in their kiss.

VLADY: Children of communism, the fucking party is over!

He takes the shoe with the bomb and holds it on his lap. He touches gently the red wire, his fingers stay on it. Jasna and Vanya look at Vlady in shock.

VANYA: Vlad, don't / touch it!

JASNA: Vlady, / what's that?

VLADY: Abandon Hope and Stupidity, All Ye who... TEN. Nine. Eight. Seven. Six.

JASNA: Vlady, this / is stupid.

VLADY: Five. Four.

VANYA: Vlad, don't do this!

VLADY: Three. Two.

VANYA: Son!

Vlady smiles. Bright glowing light.

VLADY: One.

Blackout.

END OF PLAY

ALIENS WITH EXTRAORDINARY SKILLS

Originally commissioned and developed by Women's Project and Productions, Inc. with the generous support of the New York State Council for the Arts. **Originally produced off-Broadway at Julia Miles Theatre (September-October 2008) with the following cast:**

NADIA – Natalia Payne / Marnye Young

BORAT – Seth Fischer

LUPITA – Jessica Pimentel

BOB – Kevin Isola

INS 1 – Shirine Babb

INS 2 – Gian-Murray Gianino

Directed by Tea Alagic, Scenery by Kris Stone, Costumes by Jennifer Moller

Lights by Gina Scherr, Dramaturgy by Megan E. Carter, Stage Management by Jack Gianino, Producing Artistic Director of Women's Project – Julie Crosby; Associate Producer – Allison Prouty

Special thanks for participation in the development of the play: Daniella Topol, Lark Play Development Center, New York Stage&Film, La Guardia Performing Arts Center, Shalimar Productions.

Characters:

NADIA – from Moldova, early-mid 20s

BORAT – from Russia, early-mid 30s

LUPITA – Dominican-American, late 20s

BOB – American, early-mid 30s

INS 1, INS 2 – Homeland Security (Immigration and Customs Enforcement) officers

/ - signifies the point of overlapping lines

I – A DEPORTATION LETTER

PROLOGUE

Nadia, in a clown costume, at a birthday party.

INS 1 and INS 2 are watching her.

She has two balloon animals in her hands: a dog and a squirrel.

She tells a story to the kids. She makes the balloon animals enact the story and "talk" to each other.

NADIA: And the dog said: "I'm not gonna hurt you, squirrel. Don't be afraid. Come down here, in the courtyard." And the squirrel answered: "You are a dog, dogs are scary. You bark and bite." The dog replied: "I like you, squirrel, you are pretty. I won't bite you. I want you to be my wife." The squirrel laughed: I can't marry you, dog. You are a dog, I am a squirrel. Dogs don't marry squirrels." The dog shook his head: "You're wrong. Love is love, it's the same for dogs, squirrels and all animals." "Why don't you come up here, in my tree?" – asked the squirrel – "Come up here, and I will marry you." "I wish I could" – whispered the dog. He looks up at her and cries. And cries. And cries. And out of the blue, two wings grow on the dog's back and he flies to the squirrel's tree. They laugh and play. They are happy. Very happy. But the dog can't sleep at night. He's afraid his wings will disappear. He's afraid someone will come and cut his wings.

Incision in Nadia's mind: INS 1 and INS 2 get closer.

INS 1: Homeland security.

INS 2: Immigration

INS 1: And Customs

INS 1 /INS 2: ENFORCEMENT

INS 2: Aliens are subject to mandatory detention

INS 1: If they fail to obey

INS 2 / INS 1: The rules.

INS 2: Nadia Sacharov

INS 1: You received an official LETTER

INS 1 / INS 2: Last week!

INS 2: That stated very clearly

INS 1: And politely

INS 2: That you must leave the country

INS 1: In two days

INS 2: Otherwise you're subject to

INS 1: Expedited

INS 2: Removal.

INS 1: Translation:

INS 2 / INS 2: Deportation.

Scene 1 – OUTCASTS

Nadia and Borat are waiting for the bus in an empty bus station by the road. They are dressed in clown costumes and carry suitcases. They smoke.

NADIA*(outburst):* I didn't do anything wrong! I came here on a clown visa and I am working as a clown. We are "aliens with extraordinary skills in the circus". The guy at the US Embassy was impressed with me. He said O1 visas were hard to get. I was so proud I got one. Why do they want to send us back home now? Did they change the law?

BORAT: The contracts are fake. The Romanian and the Ukrainian forged them. They created a bogus circus.

NADIA: The Magic Circus is real, it has a website!

BORAT: Did you SEE any Magic Circus?

NADIA: No, but we work as clowns. I thought it's like this. Everyone works wherever they can get work. That's what the Ukrainian told me.

BORAT: Boris and Olga work in carpentry and housecleaning.

NADIA: They just want to make more money.

BORAT: C'mon... You're not stupid.

NADIA: You knew the visas are fake and you didn't say a word?!

BORAT: You told me not to talk about bad things. You said you came to America to forget problems. You said you want new life. You said "shut up, I don't wanna hear about this!" when I showed you the article in Florida Observer. When I told you "we are in trouble"...

NADIA: There was no need to run like that. We could have packed / properly and...

BORAT: Stop it! You saw those two guys waiting for us to finish the trick and get to the "Happy Birthday" song, so they could arrest us / after.

NADIA: You see plots and catastrophes everywhere.... We're not in Soviet Union here, there is no KGB!

BORAT: Right! And we got NO deportation letter. DEPORTATION. Oh, sorry, they call it "removal procedure". We must be "removed" without delay. Or sent to prison.

Pause.

NADIA: Maybe those two guys were just... parents.

BORAT: They were Immigration Enforcement officers.

NADIA: I'm not a criminal. I don't like to run like this, through the back door... To wait here in the middle of nowhere, to go... where?... We don't even know where we are going!

BORAT: Whatever bus comes first, we take it.

NADIA: We left everything for nothing...

BORAT(*irritated, shaking her*): Do you want to end up in jail like the Romanian and the Ukrainian?

Pause.

NADIA: What's gonna happen to us?

BORAT: Look at the bright side, like the Americans say: we are in costumes, we can stop in a little town, make some money, pay for a motel or something...

NADIA: Runaways... (*slightly excited in a romantic way*) Outcasts...

BORAT: Yes. (*dramatic*) Renegados.

Pause.

NADIA: We must change our names then. I'll be... Ginger-the-Clown. You can still be Borat-the-Clown, nobody will think Borat is your real name.

BORAT: I wanna change it. I'll be ... Steve. Steve from Tennessee. Tennessee Steve. I always liked that name – Tennessee... It sounds nice.

NADIA: Let's go to Tennessee then.

BORAT: Naaah… we must go north, to a big city, so they can lose our track. *(seriously)* Or we can go back home.

NADIA: I'm not going back to Moldova! There's nobody waiting for me there.

BORAT: Niet. Daroghi nazat. *(in Russian: No, we can't go back)*

NADIA: English!

BORAT: Yes. Yes.

NADIA: You could go back to Russia.

BORAT: Sure, to become another useless drunk.

NADIA: Your mom and your sister need you there.

BORAT: Mama needs the money I send from here.

NADIA: We'll find a way to stay. We will.

BORAT: You remember Oksana? She did a formal marriage with an American. Just for the papers. She paid him 6000 dollars. It's cheaper to fall in love…

NADIA: It's BETTER to fall in love.

BORAT: That Mexican pizza guy was hot for you. And he just got his citizenship.

NADIA: I don't want pizza at my wedding. I want oysters and French champagne…

BORAT: You have a problem: you're a clown with expensive taste.

NADIA: *Tata* used to say: my girl will have the most beautiful and expensive wedding in the world! Oysters, caviar, French champagne, dancers in glowing costumes, trapeze artists pouring flowers from up in the air, colored balloons everywhere…

BORAT: Your father was something. A really good clown. Very original. When they came on tour with the Moscow Circus, I was 5 / I think…

NADIA: *Tata* was touring everywhere. Except America. He always wanted to get here "to show the Americans what the clowning ART is!" His dream was to… *(revelation)* The mug! I didn't take my mug! The one with the quote from Eleanor Roosevelt: "The future belongs to those who believe in the beauty of their dreams".

BORAT: Jesusu Kristu. Forget about stupid mug. There are mugs like that everywhere.

NADIA: I bought it from the airport. The first thing I bought with American dollars.

BORAT*(he's touched by her dreams):* You are really something. *(pause)* If I had a green card... would you marry me?

NADIA: You don't have one, so why talk about that? And you don't love me.

BORAT: I do. I love you.

NADIA: We work together. We are a team.

BORAT: Da. But you don't want to speak Russian.

NADIA: We are in America. We must speak English. Better and better and better. At home, at work, / everywhere.

BORAT: Ciort! *("damn" in Russian)* Where is that bus? We've been here for like an hour! *(beat)* I'm sick of that stupid bus. I want to drive a car.

NADIA: You don't have US driving license.

BORAT: I know this Albanian guy in Queens, New York. Cab driver. He didn't have driving license for like two years. He worked on the black market.

NADIA: Let's go to New York! I want to eat in those restaurants from "Sex and the City" where Carrie and her friends go. When I watched the series in Moldova I always covered the subtitles to practice my English.

BORAT: You're right. In New York they have many restaurants, people eat a lot, how do they say: eat OUT. And they take CABS to go out / to eat...

NADIA: They have yellow cabs!

BORAT: I think I can stay at the Albanian's... I heard he always has one or two men living in his basement and working for him. But I don't think you can't stay there.

NADIA: I'll rent something.

BORAT: You don't have money.

NADIA: I have some money. It's OK. I'll find a room. And we can work as clowns at McDonald's. In Moldova we made good money at McDonald's. The richest *siloviki* would throw parties for their kids over there. It was really fancy!

BORAT: I don't think McDonalds is so big here.

NADIA: It is! I see it advertised everywhere. We must prepare new tricks for New York. The kids are smart there. We can do the donut-chain and the dog-squirrel wedding! We should / rehearse that...

BORAT: I don't want to work as clown in New York, Nadia. Where is that bus?

NADIA: You don't want to work with me anymore?

BORAT: I just think... The Immigration guys are after us. They look for two clowns. It will be easy to find us, if we work together.

NADIA: So we should work separate?

BORAT: I'm not a good clown anyway. (*Borat walks back and forth, stopping to check if the bus is coming.*) The bus is coming! Two buses! (*beat*) You know what... It's better you take the first one, I take the second.

NADIA: I go alone?

BORAT: It's best for us. Take the bus, stop in a town, go to a cheap motel for a few days. Then come to New York. We'll talk there.

NADIA: But this is...

BORAT: Hey. You'll be fine. You're great at making those balloon animals, you can sell them. You can make money.

NADIA: I am scared.

BORAT: C'mon, GINGER! Show the Americans what clowning art is.

NADIA: Da... Yes!

BORAT*(trying to sound cheerful):* Renegados!

NADIA*(trying to sound cheerful):* Good luck, STEVE!

Nadia leaves to take the bus.

BORAT: I will call you!

INS DREAMSCAPE 1

A few minutes later. *Nadia, still dressed as a clown, is sitting in the bus.*

Incision in her mind: She's in an immigration office being interrogated by INS 1 and INS 2.

INS 1: You didn't know the visas were fake?

INS 2: Why are you lying?

INS 1: You had a small suspicion, didn't you?

INS 2: Why would someone ask for $4000 to get you a visa?

NADIA: I thought it was… to rush the process.

INS 1 / INS 2: Bribe?!

NADIA: It could take forever.

INS 2: Did you exhaust all the legal procedures?

INS 1: You didn't!

NADIA: I applied for the Visa Lottery!

INS 2: Well, what's life but a lottery.

INS 1: You must keep applying

INS 2: If you want legal status in the

INS 1 / INS 2: Unites States of America

INS 1: We are too soft

INS 2: With this interrogation.

They start rapid-fire quizzing her.

INS 1: Why did you leave your home country or country of last residence?

NADIA: My parents died. In a car crash. I sold everything. I got 8000 dollars! I paid the visa, the plane ticket… and I still have some money.

INS 2: Do you have any fear or concern about being returned to your home country?

INS 1: Or being removed from the United States?

NADIA: I don't want to be removed!

INS 2: How did you make your living in your home country?

NADIA: Family business: The SACHAROV Clowns! We were a great team! I worked as a clown since I was 6. I learned English, French, German, I can be funny in all those languages!

INS 1: Why didn't you go to Germany?

INS 2: Or France?

INS 1: You're hiding something.

INS 2: Have you ever been convicted of a felony in your country or in America?

NADIA: No!

INS 1: Have you ever plotted crimes against the United States of America?

NADIA: Never!

INS 2: Have you ever taken part in terrorist activities in your country or in America?

NADIA: God, no!

INS 1: Have you ever made plans to overthrow the United States government?

NADIA: I'm not a criminal! All I want is a normal life.

INS 1: What is a "normal life"?

INS 2: Why couldn't you have a normal life in Moldova?

INS 1: What exactly is – in your definition – a normal life?

INS 2: "Normal" – what's normal?

NADIA: To live among normal people, harmless people, free people, happy people, to like your work, to be appreciated, to have a family, a husband…

INS 1: You're saying you want an American husband?

INS 2: Why do you want an American husband?

INS 1: What's wrong with Moldovan husbands?

NADIA: I dunno … they are …

INS 1: Patronizing?

INS 2: Macho?

NADIA: A bit, yes, maybe…

INS 2: Are we talking women issues now?

INS 1: Have you ever been abused in Moldova?

INS 2: Did your man beat you? Rape you? Abuse you?

INS 1: Did your father abuse you?

NADIA: No! My father loved me! Nobody abused me there. Moldovan people are nice. Kind. Helpful. Beautiful. It's just …

INS 1 / INS 2: What?

NADIA: I couldn't make them laugh anymore. They're too poor to be happy.

INS 1 / INS 2: C'mon!

NADIA: You must understand this! Don't send me back. I want to be like you, I want to be happy! It's written in your constitution. This country is about happiness. I know that!

INS 1 and INS 2 start laughing. Scornfully.

II – TO NEW YORK, TO NEW YORK

SCENE 3

A few days later. *Spotlight on BORAT who drives a cab in New York. He talks on the cell phone.*

BORAT: There are these huge, I mean really huge, buildings. You cannot see the sky … I know you saw them on TV… Listen, Nadia, Ginger, don't expect dozens of men falling for you, it's not gonna happen. People are busy here, they work like 14-16 hours a day, they are a bit like zombies, you know... Yeah, I met lots of hot women… I just gave a ride to this girl, blonde, very pretty, she was like flirting with me all the time, from the West Village to Times Square, like really flirting, asking about my favorite food and what kinda girls I like, so in the end I asked "would you eat out with me this weekend?" She started laughing at me, like I just told some crazy funny joke, and you know what she said? "Bye. Keep the change." … Yeah, they talk with me, they smile, they make jokes, they answer the questions politely, but it's nothing there, their heart is made of ice. Snow-queens!... No, no, it's a great city, you will love it… It's colder here, take warm clothes… No, I like it, I like it a lot… *(bursting out)* How enthusiastic can I sound when I drive all nights for that fucking

Albanian who cannot speak any English but he got a

green card, and takes 80% from what I make?!

The spotlight on Borat fades.

SCENE 4

On Craigslist. Spotlights on Nadia, Lupita and Bob.

NADIA: Dear Lupita, I am interested in the room available in your apartment. I'm moving to New York City next week. Is it furnished? Where exactly is the apartment? Warm regards, Ginger.

LUPITA: Hi there. Never got "warm regards" on craigslist before. The apartment is in Washington Heights, in a 'hood full of Dominicans, on the same block with the famous *El Malecon*. I'm renting the living room. U must be clean and pay rent on time. And no smoking here, Ginger honey. "Warm regards", Lupita.

NADIA: Dear Lupita, I am very clean and reliable. How much do you ask for the room? I'm sorry but I don't know what *El Malecon* is. Yours, Ginger.

BOB: Hello there. I hear you've got a sofa 4 sale. How much?

LUPITA: Who are you, honey? Proper introduction, you know. Warm regards, Lupita.

BOB: Fucked up musician. Limited income. Gotta pay the therapy sessions. Gotta pay the divorce. My name is BOB, *te gusta*?

LUPITA: Sorry about the divorce, Bob. The sofa is green. $200. Good deal.

BOB: Can't pay more than $150, love.

NADIA: I smoke sometimes. I can quit if necessary.

LUPITA *(to Nadia)*: OK, hon. Here's the deal: $750. A big room with a high ceiling and wooden floor. Bargain!

BOB: Wanna have dinner today to negotiate further?

LUPITA: The sofa is 200. A dinner with me is $10000000, add as many zeros as you want!

BOB: Hot, hot, hot ☺

LUPITA *(to Nadia)*: Ginger, u American?

BOB: Last offer: 160 and a priceless dinner with The BOB. "Eat what you can" (: Smiley face.

LUPITA: U have some nerve, man! I can see why your wife divorced u. Here's the deal: 180 – "eat" it or leave it.

NADIA: Ginger is a stage name. My birth name is Nadia.

LUPITA: U actress? Me too.

NADIA: I am a clown.

LUPITA: Cool! Are you Russian or Romanian like that gymnast?

BOB: OK, Lupi. You win. $180. See you tomorrow, love.

NADIA: I'm from Moldova. My father was Russian, my mother was Romanian. They are dead.

LUPITA: Oh, sorry to hear that, honey. Sad face. ;(

BOB: Tomorrow, after work, 6 pm – cool, Lupi?

LUPITA: So u take the room, Ginger? I kinda feel it's gonna be fun to be roommates.

NADIA: We can be like sisters. When can I move in?

LUPITA: Thursday. I'm free on Thursday.

NADIA: OK! I'll be in New York on Thursday!

LUPITA: Looking fwd to see u. Haven't seen a clown since I was 5 back home in the DR. No offense, hon. Any other questions?

NADIA: What is *El Malecon*?

LUPITA: A restaurant, girl. Good breakfast, eggs, juices, fried cheese, mangu. Homemade, tasty, reminds me of my grandma's kitchen. I hope you like *cafe con leche* and mashed plantains.

BOB: Lupiiiiiiiiiiitaaaaa!

LUPITA: Not good tomorrow, Bobby. Thursday. Lunchtime. Have all the money ready. Cash.

BOB: OK! Lunch at your place. Yummy. I'll take the afternoon off ☺

LUPITA: Don't get excited. My roommate will be here too.

BOB: A threesome-dessert?

LUPITA: U a perv, Bobby-boy?

BOB: Just kidding. Sense of humor having a nap?

LUPITA: U better take a nap yourself, u tired from jerking off.

BOB: Ha, ha, ha ☺

NADIA: I love *café con leche*! We call it *cafea cu lapte*. Mama used to make it too.

LUPITA: Thursday. 1 pm. Don't be late, smiley-face.

SCENE 5

Thursday. *Lupita's living room. Lupita speaks on her cell phone.*

LUPITA: Yes, come in an hour or so! … I don't care you're already in my 'hood, I can't deal with you right now, my roommate is moving in … I don't know, go kill some time in a bar, in a restaurant, go to *El Malecon*!... *(the bell rings)* There she is! Gotta go now. *(she hangs up)* I can't believe this guy!

She opens the door to Nadia, who carries a small suitcase.

NADIA: Hi. Lupita?

LUPITA: Hi! Ginger, yes? (*Nadia nods*) Let me help you.

NADIA: No, no, it's fine.

LUPITA: Come in! Come!

Nadia enters the living room, puts the suitcase down and looks around.

LUPITA: It's a big apartment. You know, for 750, you generally get some shit hole with no windows and a shared bathroom in the hallway. This is the very best you can get for this money, trust me, you're really lucky, sister! (*beat*) So… do you like the city?

NADIA: It has a… special energy … I feel like nothing bad can happen to me here, like it's impossible to die here.

LUPITA: That's an intense way to put it. Yeah, New York is great, honey, the perfect city for people like us, working in the entertainment industry.

NADIA: I don't work in the … entertainment industry, I'm just a clown, (*making a face*) funny-ha-ha.

LUPITA: That's entertainment industry, honey. Don't sell yourself short. Here you gotta learn to be confident, assertive. New Yorkers are tough.

NADIA *(inspecting the sofa):* This is where I'm gonna sleep?

LUPITA: Generally people like to bring their own bed...

NADIA *(pointing at the suitcase):* That's all I have.

LUPITA: Wanna buy a bed? There are some cheap ones around the corner at Jose's store.

NADIA: No, it's OK. I can sleep on the sofa.

LUPITA: That sucks, girl! I'm selling this sofa. I thought whoever moves in wanna have a bed or something. I have this guy, Bob, coming over to buy it in like half-hour.

NADIA *(trying to seem tough):* Then what, am I to sleep on the floor? I mean, for this money, I mean ... you should provide a bed. In Florida / I had...

LUPITA: For this money, you have a big room, access to the kitchen, to the bathroom, you have TV, video,

DVD, *(looking Nadia in the eyes)* someone who doesn't ask questions about papers and other shit like that...

Nadia goes to the window to avoid a discussion about papers.

LUPITA: Plus a window with a nice view!

NADIA: You can't see the sky.

LUPITA: But you can see that awesome courtyard and the little garden. Flowers, and a tree! Where else in Manhattan can you get that?

NADIA: Why is the dumpster there?

LUPITA: OK, you don't like this, you don't like that, fine. There are many others in line for this room, you know. I got a guy who'd pay 800!

NADIA: No! I'm taking it! I was just ... No, it's fine, I'm moving in. Here's the money. 750 dollars.

She takes a bundle of money out of her purse. She counts 750 dollars and hands it to Lupita.

LUPITA: That's the deposit. I also need the rent for the first month.

Nadia counts another 750 dollars. What's left is about $200. She gives the money to Lupita.

NADIA: Here.

LUPITA: Listen, Ginger… I can help you buy a cheap futon.

NADIA (*trying to sound optimistic*): It's OK, I can sleep on the floor…

LUPITA: *Dios mió*, that's not gonna happen in my apartment. It's New York here, honey, not my grandma's village in the old DR. I'll buy you a cheap futon after that Bob pays for the sofa.

NADIA (*sitting on the sofa*): Why are you selling it?

LUPITA: Why am I selling it? Because it's kinda crammed over here and if you had any furniture I would have to … Right. Why am I selling it?! (*beat*) Damn, girl, now I have to have lunch with that Bob. *Nadia takes a balloon out of her pocket and starts blowing it and twisting it, making a balloon animal.*

LUPITA: I don't trust this guy. Craigslist is like a magnet for weirdoes. I'm lucky with you though. (*looking at the balloon*) Right? You could have been a horny dyke or some pathological nuts… OK. Make yourself comfortable. Unpack, do your thing…

Lupita goes offstage. Nadia is twisting the balloon. Lupita comes back with a jacket and the NYC Guide.

LUPITA: Here, the New York City Guide. With pictures. Maps. Everything. Take a look.

NADIA: I can't believe I'm in New York. Do you watch "Sex and the City"?

LUPITA: What, the reruns? It's a silly show, it's not about women like us … *(about the balloon)* What's that? An umbrella?

NADIA *(handing her the shape she's made)*: A flower.

LUPITA: Wow. It's… nice. Never got one of these… *(she takes the keys out of her jacket's pocket and hands them to Nadia)* Here are your keys.

She's ready to leave.

NADIA: Thanks. Where are you going?

LUPITA: To cancel the deal so you can have the sofa. The guy is waiting at *El Malecon*. Wish me luck!

NADIA: I'm sorry, I … I didn't want to create any problems.

LUPITA: Chill, will you, roommate? Consider the problem solved.

Lupita leaves. Nadia opens the New York City Guide.

INS DREAMSCAPE 2

NADIA *(reading):* Eyewitness. Travel Guide. NEW YORK. Architecture. Restaurants. Walks. Museums. Hotels. Shopping. Theatres. Maps. "The Guides That Show You What Others Only Tell You".

Incision in Nadia's mind. *The INS spring out of the New York City Guide.*

INS 1: Eyewitness.

INS 2: Travel Guide.

INS 1: Eyewitness!

INS 2: Travel Guide!

INS 1 / INS 2: New York area by area.

INS 1: Introducing New York

INS 2: To Nadia!

INS 1: Introducing Nadia

INS 2: To New York!

INS 1 *(menacingly)*: Before

INS 2: We REMOVE her

INS 1: From this country.

INS 2: Translation:

INS 1 / INS 2: DEPORTATION.

NADIA *(reading):* From its first sighting almost 500 years ago by Giovanni da Varrazano, New York's harbor was the prize that all of Europe wanted to capture. The Dutch first sent fur traders to the area in 1621.

INS 1: But they lost the colony they called New Amsterdam.

INS 2: To the English in 1664.

NADIA: The settlement was rechristened New York.

INS 1: And the name stayed.

INS 2: And people started to come.

INS 1: Immigrants.

INS 2: Thousands of immigrants.

INS 1: Seeking a better life.

INS 2: Overpopulation.

INS 1: Many living in slums.

NADIA *(reading):* The mix of cultures has enriched the city. And became its defining quality.

INS 1: East Village!

As INS 1 and INS 2 become absorbed by their new roles as "tour guides" and stop paying attention to Nadia, she runs away and hides in the audience.

INS 2: The Tenement Museum.

INS 1: Newcomers lived here.

INS 2: 6-8 people in a room.

INS 1: Big families.

INS 2: Life is tough.

They notice Nadia's absence.

INS 1: Where is the girl?

INS 2: The girl has disappeared!

INS 1*(asking the audience):* Where is she?

INS 1 / INS 2: Nadia!

INS 1: Where are you?

INS 2 *(asking a woman in the audience):* Have you seen her?

INS 1: It's a felony. To help an illegal immigrant, you know.

INS 2: An illegal alien.

INS 1: People do so many crazy things.

INS 2: For love, many times they do them for love.

INS 1: Other times, for pleasure.

INS 2: Out of compassion.

INS 1: Fear

INS 2: Curiosity

INS 1: Boredom

INS 2: Insecurity

INS 1: Need for power

INS 2: Sadism slash masochism

INS 1: Who knows why

INS 2 / INS 1: People do things.

INS 2(*to a member of the audience*): Did you help her disappear?

INS 1: I hope you didn't do that.

INS 2: That would be such a shame.

INS 1: We would have to arrest you.

INS 2: We don't want to arrest you.

INS 1: But if we must…

INS 2: We must.

They "arrest" a member of the audience and talk to her/him.

INS 1: She's from Moldova, you know.

INS 2: The unhappiest country in the world.

INS 1: I read that.

INS 2: In "The Geography of Bliss".

INS 1: What about you? Are you happy?

INS 2: Unhappy?

INS 1: We can make you very unhappy, you know.

INS 2: Or very happy.

INS 1: It's up to you.

INS 2: Your choice.

NADIA: I'm here! Leave her/him alone! They didn't help me. Nobody helped me. You want me, I'm here.

INS 1: There she is. Our little alien.

INS 2: Don't disappear in another dimension again!

They laugh and get her.

SCENE 6

Later, that Thursday, in Lupita's apartment. Nadia has just made a new balloon animal. Lupita enters with BOB who carries a bunch of beers. One can tell they had some drinks before.

LUPITA: Ginger, honey! I brought a guest. I couldn't get rid of him.

BOB: Hi.

NADIA: Hi.

LUPITA: He's the guy who wanted to buy the sofa.

BOB: I still want it.

LUPITA: We went through that like forty times already. Ginger needs the sofa to sleep on it. Period. *(pointing at his head)* Are you slow or what?

BOB *(to Nadia):* See what are you doing to me?

NADIA: I'm sorry, / but…

LUPITA: You don't need to explain anything to him, honey. It's my sofa. I made a decision. I feel like 2 percents guilty coz I did promise it to him but we're gonna have a beer together and that's that. I won't feel guilty anymore.

BOB *(to Nadia):* I bought a couple of beers…

LUPITA: Yes, he bought them.

BOB *(to Nadia):* To celebrate your moving in.

LUPITA: He's a sweet talker.

NADIA: I don't really drink beer…

LUPITA: You gotta try one of these.

BOB *(to Nadia, about the balloon):* What's that, a duck?

NADIA *(surprised he got it):* Yes. The ugly duckling.

BOB: He's not ugly.

Lupita throws herself onto the sofa.

LUPITA: OK, Bobby, take a freakin' seat and open the beers for us. Relaxation time! My night off.

Bob opens the beers, hands one to Lupita and one to Nadia and sits on the sofa, next to Lupita. He opens a beer for himself.

Nadia feels awkward sitting next to him and sits on a chair. They sip their beers.

LUPITA *(to Nadia)*: Bob has some very interesting theories about love and foreign women. You gotta hear this.

BOB: No, I don't feel / like…

LUPITA: C'mon, Bobby-boy, you talked non-stop for the last – what? – three hours, and now you're silent all of a sudden.

NADIA: It's OK, I don't need to / hear…

LUPITA: Tell her what you told your shrink. It's funny!

NADIA: Really, I don't want to…

LUPITA: It's good for our self-esteem. Listen to him.

He gestures towards Bob to start the "show".

BOB: OK. So… I went to my shrink last week, she's this upscale woman in her 50s… And she's like "why do you date women whose mother tongue is not English, Bob?" And I'm like: You're a shrink, haven't you noticed? When you are forced to pay closer attention to people's words, you actually communicate better. If you both speak English and you both think you know what you're talking about, there's all this room for misinterpretation about what's actually being said. But if you are not sure that the other person is getting you, you check her out, you make sure she gets you. And if… if she's not sure she's getting you, she checks you out, you know, she pays attention, until she gets you… And even the silences begin to have some meaning, you know, because you're used to paying attention to each other…

LUPITA *(to Nadia):* See?

BOB: On my tours with the band, we had groupies, fans, all that. We traveled abroad: Mexico, Eastern Europe, Russia… And believe me, those girls were really paying attention to us. Not just as musicians: as men, as people…

LUPITA *(to Nadia):* I've never dated a musician. They're not reliable.

BOB: Then I married this waspy Upper West Side girl and everything fucking changed. She got me a office job at her dad's company. I tried to talk to her. In our

mutual language – English. Did she get what I said?
No. Nothing. Nada.

LUPITA *(laughing):* Nada!

BOB: Look at me now. I don't go on tours anymore. My pals gave up on me. I stopped playing music when I became that shitty office rat... Of course she kicked me out of the apartment. Had a better lawyer. And you know what, as fucked up as that may sound, I'm OK with this new situation. I don't wanna do anything for a while. Just … live. Gimme a bunch of beers to keep me company and I'm happy these days. I got this cool little job at Video&Music Rentals. I'm doing my little thing… And you know something else, I said: I can't afford these therapy sessions. You take less than my last shrink, but still … I'm outta here. It was only 7 minutes, wasn't it? Twenty bucks should do it.

LUPITA: Now we are your shrinks, Bobby. Fifty bucks should do it!

Lupita and Bob are laughing. Bob opens more beers.

BOB: Cheers! To foreign women! To Lupita, the hottest mamacita! *(singing)* Ma-ma-cita!

LUPITA: Cheers!

BOB *(to Nadia):* In Russian you say… I know… Nazdarovje!

NADIA: Cheers.

III – THE CITY NEVER SLEEPS

SCENE 7

A few days later. Borat and Nadia talk on the phone. Nadia is at home, has the phone on speaker. Borat is in the cab. Nadia is twisting a balloon while talking. There are few balloon animals around her.

BORAT: What did you expect, a palace? This is New York, be happy you don't have to sleep in a storage room. And you say this girl Lupita is really nice.

NADIA: She's great. Very… how do Americans say? When you are like really energetic and full of life…

BORAT: Outrageous. They say "outrageous".

NADIA: No, I think it's "outgoing".

BORAT: That's when you go out a lot.

NADIA: You're wrong. Anyway. Lupita is nice and sexy and has this great positive energy. Like she's really happy all the time. And she dresses well.

BORAT: So you're all set. Welcome to New York! The city that never sleeps! Is she legal?

NADIA: She has the lease in her name, so she must be.

BORAT: Ask her. Find out how she got her green card.

NADIA: I don't wanna think about that now. I've had an awful headache the whole day. A... (trying to remember the word) hangover.

BORAT: But you don't drink much. You went to a party or something?

NADIA: We had some beers here, in the apartment. Too many.

BORAT: So you're having fun, huh?

NADIA: I wouldn't call it fun.

BORAT: So you didn't do anything the whole day...

NADIA: I explored the city. I walked more than 100 blocks.

BORAT: Like you're on a tourist visa or something.

NADIA: OK. Good night.

BORAT: C'mon, Nadia! It's the Albanian's cell phone, we can talk the whole night if we want.

NADIA: I'm tired. And I'm Ginger!

BORAT: Don't hang up on me! Listen! Nadia?! Ginger?

NADIA: What?

BORAT: So... What's this girl Lupita doing for living?

NADIA: She works in a club in Queens.

BORAT: Waitress?

NADIA: No, in the... entertainment industry.

BORAT: Which club?

NADIA: I dunno. "Pink" something.

BORAT: Hot Pink Pussycat?!

NADIA: Yeah. You know it?

BORAT: I drive by it everyday!

NADIA: I hear it's a cool club.

BORAT: You wanna work there too?!

NADIA *(laughing):* I'm not hot enough.

BORAT: Is that Lupita a super-hottie?

NADIA: Why are you so interested in Lupita?

BORAT: Just… you know. It's not like I'm having lots of fun these days. Living in the Albanian's basement with other six guys… Sleeping on a mattress… When can I visit you?

NADIA: That's not a good idea, STEVE. You know that.

BORAT *(after an awkward silence):* So… that Lupita is a stripper or what?

NADIA: She's a performer. An exotic dancer. She's gonna make it far, she's really tough and determined.

BORAT *(joking):* Yeah, sure, far like … New Jersey!

NADIA: Oh, shut up. You don't understand big dreams. You don't LOVE to do anything.

BORAT *(laughing):* I love to drive and drink vodka and make out with a hot woman, all at the same time, if possible. I used to do / that, back home in…

NADIA: I waste my time talking with you. I gotta go.

BORAT (to Nadia): OK, OK, don't go. (to the man in the cab) Here? (he pulls up the car) Thank you, sir! Have a great night!

NADIA: You shouldn't talk on the cell phone when you're driving.

BORAT: This guy left me a huge tip. Eight bucks! It was 12 dollars and he gave me 20. A true gentleman. A businessman. He looks like he owns half of Manhattan. Had this golden ring, like HUGE, on his little finger... You gotta marry this kinda guy, Nadia, it's your best chance. These guys have horse power, they make a call and your green card lands in your mailing box. Your goal should be to meet / this kinda guy.

NADIA: OK. I'm really going to bed now. I had a long day.

She hangs up. She looks at the shape she made: a nice squirrel.

BORAT: C'mon, it's New York! You don't go to sleep at 10 pm! ... Nadia? ... Ginger? ... *(to another driver: "Moron" in Russian)* Durak!

Lights shift to a men-only club's dressing room. Lupita, wearing a sexy skin-revealing cowgirl outfit, is contemplating herself in the mirror.

LUPITA: You look good, girl! Those sweaty pigs don't deserve you. They don't deserve looking at you. Stick that into your mind. You gonna go out there and PERFORM! It's a performance, a role you play. You gotta be good at it. If you're good in this role, you'll be excellent in any others. OK. Warm up exercises. *(she starts swaying her body in a sexy way).* You're good. A professional must be good in any circumstances. Remember that. Tell that to yourself everyday in the mirror. You are awesome! They don't deserve you! You will finish acting school and go on Broadway, girl! You'll see the name Lupita in big glowing letters. You'll go to Hollywood. You'll walk on the red carpet with Antonio Banderas. You'll be a star! You ARE a star but people don't know it yet. But they will. They will!

SCENE 8

Later that night. LUPITA *is dancing around a pole for Borat, who's sitting in a comfortable chair, sipping vodka.*

BORAT: Yeah, baby! …. Yeah!

LUPITA: Whadda you say you do, honey?

BORAT: I'm a … doctor.

LUPITA: Oh, yeah. What's your name, doctor? Where are you from, doctor?

BORAT: Steve. Steve from Tennessee.

LUPITA: C'mon, where are you really from?

BORAT: What do you mean?

LUPITA: Oh, yeah. What do I mean. I mean I don't care, Steve. Here you can be whoever you wanna be.

BORAT *(she makes some very sexy moves):* Oh, God! What are you doing?

LUPITA: I start from the top and I weeee my way down…

BORAT: Wow!

LUPITA: Do you like that, honey?

BORAT: God, yes! I'm not sorry for the 50 bucks.

LUPITA: You were worried you paid too much, doctor?

BORAT: No, 50 dollars is nothing for me. I mean… I don't mean to offend you … I'm rich. I'm very rich. I'm Donald Trump of… horse doctors.

LUPITA: Oh, yeah? Horse doctor? I like horses. Great to meet you, "Donald".

BORAT: Horses are good, how do you say, reliable, horses are reliable animals. I help them. Yes, I'm a good horse doctor. Ay, that was nice! Do it again! Ride me, baby! Ride me!

LUPITA: "Horse doctor"… You're not a Russian spy, are you?

BORAT: Why do you say that? I'm not Russian.

LUPITA: I know accents. I'm an actress. But don't worry, honey, (musically) here you can be whoever you wanna be, Steve-from-Tennessee.

BORAT: You are smart for a pro… professional actress, I mean.

LUPITA *(stops dancing):* I'm not a whore, vodka-boy. Stick that into your mind.

BORAT: Please don't stop!

LUPITA: I'm done. That's what you get for 50 bucks, honey.

BORAT closes his eyes and puts a hand on his crotch.

LUPITA: What are you doing?

BORAT: I'm going to rub my penis to the good memories of you dancing.

LUPITA: Are you crazy? You can't jerk off here. Go to the bathroom! Open your eyes and go to the fucking bathroom!

BORAT *(with his eyes closed, his hands up to show her he's not touching himself):* OK, I'm going to imagine that I rub my penis to the good memories of you dancing.

LUPITA: I forbid you to imagine anything about me!

BORAT: You can't do that. The dance was yours, the good memories are mine.

LUPITA: Open your eyes!

BORAT *(with his eyes closed)*: Wow, that was nice! Do it again!

LUPITA: Loco! *(crazy in Spanish)*

BORAT *(with his eyes closed)*: Hmmm… You are beautiful, mamacita, you damn are.

LUPITA: OK. How do you say "whatever" in Russian?

BORAT: Ja t'bia lublu! *("I love you")*

LUPITA: I'm done here.

She's ready to exit.

BORAT *(opening his eyes)*: Wait! I lied. I'm not a horse doctor.

LUPITA: Whatever.

BORAT: I'm a cab driver.

LUPITA *(mockingly)*: Great!

She's not really upset but intrigued by the guy. He's quite different from the usual clients. He's kinda fun, in a weird way, of course.

BORAT: Can I drive you home after work?

LUPITA: Nope.

BORAT: Tomorrow?

LUPITA: No.

BORAT: On weekend?

LUPITA: How do you say "never" in Russian?

She exits, smiling like "I can't believe this guy".

IV – WHAT'S IN A NAME

SCENE 9

Three weeks later. *Around 6 pm. Lupita's and Nadia's apartment.*
A fancy shoebox is on the sofa. Balloon toys are on the floor. Lupita tries a pair of shoes and walks around the living room. Nadia has just finished making a balloon horse.

NADIA: Columbus Circle is a good spot. I like it there. It's near the park and I can just stand by the statue and twist balloons. Squirrels sell the best. Five bucks. Dogs are the cheapest: only two bucks. It's easy to make them. Horses are three bucks. They're actually dogs with longer neck. I made 190 dollars last week! And 175 the week before.

LUPITA: It doesn't seem like a good spot. (*kicking a balloon animal*) This living room has turned into a rubber zoo. You'd make more money twisting condoms!

They laugh. Nadia crams the balloon animals under the sofa. She looks at Lupita with admiration.

NADIA: Are they really Manolo Blahnik?

LUPITA: Of course. What kinda silly question is that? Look at the label. I paid 725 bucks for them.

NADIA: Wow.

LUPITA: Yeah. My tips for a week.

NADIA: That's... lots of money.

LUPITA: I deserve them. I work hard.

NADIA: You look gorgeous.

LUPITA: I must. (*beat*) Hey, wanna try them on?

NADIA: They're yours, I can't ...

LUPITA: C'mon, try them on, we have the same size!

NADIA (*excited*): OK!

She tries them on and walks the way Lupita did.

NADIA: I will never afford such shoes.

LUPITA: Never say "never", sis. You gotta work on your self-esteem and the success will come. When you look in the mirror – what do you tell yourself?

NADIA: Nothing.

LUPITA: You gotta talk to yourself, honey. Stuff like: I'm gonna make it, I know I'm gonna make it. I will …. such and such, whatever you dream to be. Working on your self-esteem, hon, that's the way to go.

NADIA: But I do have self-esteem. I like what I do. I only need to make more money.

LUPITA: Don't forget your rent is due on Monday. I mean I'm cool and nice, I like you and all that but you gotta pay the rent on time, honey. I don't run a charity business here.

NADIA: I will pay. I will work hard this weekend, I will.

LUPITA: You mean you don't have the money?

NADIA: Not yet.

LUPITA: And how exactly do you plan to find work?

NADIA: This weekend I'll dress as a clown and go to the McDonald's in Harlem. I'll make tricks for the kids. I'll pass the hat… I'm sure I'll get hired for some birthday parties. I'm cheap, for 80 dollars they get lots of fun out of me.

LUPITA: You won't make the 750 for the rent then.

NADIA: I will. I will work the whole weekend.

LUPITA: Girl, I'm sorry to sound like a bitch, but you won't make that kinda money doing tricks for some kids at McDonald's. You gotta find some rich clients, you gotta be invited to the Upper West Side or Long Island. That's where you make money, not in Central Park. *(Nadia takes the shoes off)* Put them in the box. *(Nadia puts the shoes in the box).*

Look, me, I got three gigs on Friday night and Friday is my big money night at the club with three of my big clients plus my new regular – a silly guy from "Tennessee". So, I can't take this gig at a party in Soho where a friend recommended me.

NADIA: I can go in your place! Can I go in your place?

LUPITA: It's an adults-only party.

NADIA: I can create new tricks for adults. All adults have an inner child.

LUPITA: Girl … You're not right for this gig. You haven't done this kinda stuff before. OK, it's no sex involved and no stripping, but you might have to slap a hand or two that gropes your ass, you know.

NADIA: You haven't seen me working, I'm really tough when it comes to work.

LUPITA: I dunno … If you go, you gotta keep your wits about you. You gotta be careful. Don't drink no shit they give you.

NADIA: I come from a country with heavy vodka drinkers…

LUPITA: I dunno… You will freak out when some sweaty guy shouts: c'mon, shake it, baby, shake it!

NADIA: I can shake it, I can.

She stars swaying her body in a sexy way, she's funny rather than sexy.

LUPITA: You're as sexy as a pumpkin. *(she gets up and starts moving in a very sexy way)* See, you gotta sway your hips like this!

NADIA *(moving better):* Look! I can do it!

LUPITA *(sitting):* You're a clown. Stick to that, girl.

NADIA: Please, Lupi! Just this time, get me this gig! Those people might have kids, they'll see what I can do and invite me to kids parties, I'm very good, they will like me, you'll / see!

LUPITA: I don't like this. You gotta figure out a way to make money to pay your rent. You can't rely on me to help with that. I work hard to pay my bills ON TIME. Last year I was short on money and I got an eviction notice. I can't let that happen anymore. I took the job at the club and I was never late on rent ever since.

NADIA: I'm sorry ... I / will (find a way to pay)...

LUPITA: They sent the "Five Day Notice" 7 times, in English and Spanish. It scared the shit outta me. This is a tough city, you know.

NADIA: I know.

LUPITA: No, you don't. Do you know why I'm renting the living room?

NADIA: For money?

LUPITA: I'm renting the living room so I can work at the club only until midnight instead of 2 am. I'm renting the living room to save money for acting classes.

NADIA: Then let me go to this party! I have to make money. I won't ask for any other gigs. Please, please. Only this time. I promise / I will…

LUPITA: OK, OK … Calm down. *(beat)* I guess it can't be too bad, Soho people are classy: middle-aged businessmen and older artsy guys who like fancy food and exotic dancers… There was this belly dancer from Morocco, Isset, they worshipped her. She ended up with a divorced lawyer in his late 50s who got her a house in the Hamptons and now she's sorta running his "bed&breakfast"… *(Lupita laughs. Nadia is relieved, she laughs too.)*

Maybe you'll find your Mr Big over there.

NADIA: My Mr Big should be a perfect gentleman. Totally in love with me. Making coffee for both of us in the morning. The most perfect coffee in the world. Not too sweet, not too strong. Just the way I like it…

LUPITA: There's plenty of Starbucks boys.

They laugh. The bell rings.

LUPITA: That crazy Bob again. Can't he give us a day off? *(ring)* He should pay rent for the time he spends over here.

NADIA: I'll get it!

Nadia goes offstage and comes back with Bob who carries 12 cans of beer.

BOB: Ladies, wait no longer, The Bob has arrived!

LUPITA: Bobby-Beer-Can himself.

BOB: Am I disturbing?

LUPITA: As always.

BOB: I knew you missed me.

LUPITA: You wanna move in here? There's some room in the closet.

BOB: Can I take a seat on MY sofa?

LUPITA: That's a stupid question. We know you will anyway.

Bob throws himself onto the sofa and opens a beer can.

LUPITA: Rude Boy, throw one over!

Bob throws her a can. Nadia is still standing.

BOB: C'mon, Ginger, don't be shy, come sit here!

Nadia goes and sits on the sofa next to Bob. He hands her a beer can.

BOB: Guess what, gals. I'm starting to learn Russian. I watched Russian movies all day at work: Tarkovski, Mihalkov. Really cool movies. Do you know those directors, Ginger?

NADIA: Yeah. I can't watch those movies anymore, they're too depressing.

BOB: C'mon, all great art is born out of depression!

LUPITA: Now he's giving us the philosophy of depression. I don't wanna hear that.

Bob takes a balloon out of his bag and starts twisting it. Nadia is impressed but hides it.

BOB: Have you been to Brighton Beach, gals?

LUPITA: We don't have time for the beach.
Remember that "obscene" four letter word: WORK.

BOB: I know, I know. I'm just saying. Ginger, you gotta see those Russians walking on the promenade with the whole family. We don't do that here in America. We walk our dogs, yes, but that's not the same. They walk their kids, their grandparents… I like that. It feels real.

LUPITA: Move to Brighton Beach, Bobby. Go smell the ocean and give us a break.

BOB: I would. But my job is here, around the corner, Lupi.

LUPITA: Nobody's paying you for the extra hours HERE.

Bob has made a dog.

BOB: It's all I can make… Sparky the Dog. Woof-woof. *(he hands it to Nadia)* Doesn't bite.

NADIA *(to Bob, about the dog):* It's good.

LUPITA: Now he starts with balloon animals too … Baloney! Both of you. Go sell them and make some money.

BOB (*mockingly*): Right. It's time to change my career. Bob-the-beer-drinking-clown!

Nadia sips from her beer. The dog balloon is in her lap. They all drink.

LUPITA: Bobby-boy, prove yourself useful, honey. Go make me a little cuppa joe. I gotta leave for work in like an hour. Damn, I really don't feel like moving my ass today.

Bob heads for the kitchen.

BOB: You want a cuppa coffee, Ginger?

INS DREAMSCAPE IV

Incision in Nadia's mind: INS 1 *and* INS 2 *show up.*
Nadia has the balloon dog in her arms.

INS 1 (*mocking her*): You want a cuppa coffee, "Ginger"?

INS 2: I make perfect coffee, "Ginger"!

NADIA (*"threatening" them with the balloon dog*): Woof-woof! Go away!

They laugh. Then become menacing.

INS 2: Tell the truth!

INS 1: You wanna go to that party

INS 2: To find a rich guy.

INS 1 / INS 2: Mr Big?! *(they laugh)*

INS 1: Yeah, marry Mr Big!

INS 2: For the money.

NADIA: I don't care about money!

INS 1: You should!

INS 2: Marry Mr Big!

INS 1: For the house.

INS 2: In the Hamptons.

NADIA: No!

INS 1 / INS 2: Oh, yes.

NADIA *("threatening" them with the balloon dog)*: Go!

Woof-Woof!

INS 2 *(mocking her)*: Oh, scary!

INS 1: We know what all this is about.

They start rapid-fire talking to her.

INS 2: It's for the green card.

INS 1: We know that trick.

INS 2: It doesn't work!

INS 1: It's WRONG.

INS 2: We know: when you feel the "greencard" pressure, you can't think about love.

INS 1: Even when it is love.

INS 2: You can't see it.

INS 1: This word, love, translates for you as "legal".

INS 2: You put love in your pocket

INS 1: You mix it with a City Hall ceremony and a dress

INS 2: A wedding dress

INS 1: Not a white one

INS 2: You don't deserve a white one

INS 1: You're a criminal after all

INS 2: When you say "I do" you mean "I do what I can to make you laugh and to make me stay."

INS 1: That's the dynamic.

INS 2: You put a marriage in your pocket and take out a green card.

INS 1: That's the trick.

NADIA: I hate this trick!

INS 2: Clowns are not allowed to hate tricks.

INS 1: That's what you do for a living.

SCENE 10

A cab parked in a dark empty tree-lined street. Lupita sits next to Borat, in the front seat.

LUPITA *(a bit scared)*: Why did you stop?

BORAT: Look! It's full moon. Beautiful perfect round moon.

LUPITA: Yes...

BORAT: I need to show you something. A surprise.

LUPITA: I need to get home.

BORAT: Don't be scared. You will get home.

LUPITA: It's late.

BORAT: Didn't I drive you home everyday for the last three weeks? You can trust me. I'm not a freak.

LUPITA *(still tensed)*: What do you wanna show me?

BORAT: Close your eyes.

LUPITA: Oh, no, I'm not gonna close my eyes.

BORAT: Then put your hands on your eyes. Like this.

(he shows her)

LUPITA: I don't really…

BORAT: I can't do the surprise if you look at me. I need to change into something.

LUPITA: What? A vampire?

BORAT: OK. If you want to look, you look. Watch this.

She closes her eyes.

LUPITA: OK. You have one minute to "change". I'm counting. One. Two. Three. Four. …

Borat takes a red clown nose out of his pocket and a few fluorescent flowers sticks. He sticks them onto the windshield. He takes a few nice candles out of a plastic bag and lights them with his lighter.

LUPITA: I'm opening my eyes!

BORAT: Don't look! One more minute…

LUPITA: No. *(she opens her eyes)*

BORAT *(wearing the red clown nose, starts singing - he can't really sing)*:

Happy Full-Moon,

Happy Full-Night,

LU-PI-TA!

I wanna hold you tight

I wanna say Good-Night,

LU-PI-TA!

You are my dream come true

You are my fairy-LU

You are my moon, my star,

You are, You are...

LU-PIIIIII-TA!

She laughs. He's ready to kiss her.

BORAT: I'm dying to kiss you.

LUPITA: Not with that red nose on you!

They laugh, looking at each other.

SCENE 11

*Nadia's and Lupita's apartment. **Friday evening**.*

Nadia is wearing a very sexy clown costume, adding the last details.

Bob sits on the sofa, drinking a Guinness beer and twisting a balloon.

Nadia looks at Bob from time to time, to check if he finds her sexy.

BOB *(humming):* Finally alone with you, baby…
Finally alone with you…

NADIA *(trying to act tough)*: I told you not to wait for Lupi. She might get home tomorrow morning.

BOB: I don't mind waiting. I still have four more beers to drink.

NADIA: Our apartment is not your private bar.

BOB: "Our" apartment?

NADIA: I pay rent for this room. Everything in here is MINE.

BOB *(joking)*: Then I'm yours too. Not that I mind that. I don't mind hanging out here. With you. With you wearing that ridiculous outfit. What is that?

NADIA: You don't have to like it. It's for a fancy party in Soho. I'll provide the entertainment. Lupita recommended me.

She practices some choreography/movement.

BOB: No kidding?

NADIA: Guess how much they pay – 250 dollars per hour! In three hours I make the money for the rent.

BOB: You'll have to strip, won't you?

NADIA: No!

BOB: You'll have to strip.

NADIA: You like to annoy me. Get up and go home!

BOB: I'm waiting for my "girlfriend" Lupita.

NADIA: Lupi is not your girlfriend.

BOB: You're jealous. Tell the truth. You want me to join you at the party? To be your bodyguard? Your pimp?

NADIA: Shut up!

BOB: Your lover?

NADIA: You know what: I'm gonna ignore you from now on. You don't exist. You're a piece of furniture. A blanket on the sofa. A Guinness can.

BOB: You sure you don't need a ride to the party?

NADIA: You don't have a car!

BOB: An A train ride. I can walk you to the subway.

NADIA: I'll take a cab. They pay for a cab.

She puts on the pair of Manolo Blahnik shoes.

BOB: Designer shoes!? Where did you get those? They don't match your silly outfit.

NADIA *(proudly)*: Manolo Blahnik. Real Manolo Blahniks.

BOB: They're Lupita's, aren't they?

NADIA: She said I could borrow them. It's my debut in New York.

Bob has made a balloon squirrel.

He checks on Nadia to see if she noticed the work.

He hands the squirrel to Nadia.

BOB: I'm getting better at this.

Nadia ignores it. But she likes it. She heads to the door. She walks sexy, swaying her hips, trying to get into the new "role".

NADIA *(flirtatiously)*: I'm outta here. I'm wanted to the most perfect New Yorkers party! No access for losers like you. Bye, sofa blanket! Shut the door when you leave. And don't fall asleep on MY sofa!

Bob writes something on a piece of paper and runs after her.

BOB: Hey, Ginger! Here's my cell phone number, call me if… you need a ride, a walk to the subway, I dunno, anything. Just don't be shy, call me.

Nadia takes the paper, puts it provocatively in her bra, and leaves.

SCENE 12

A cab parked in a dark empty tree-lined street. **Friday night, around 2 am.**

Lupita and Borat are making out on the back seat.

Lupita whispers "Steve" in Borat's ear. *Borat wants more, Lupita stops him.*

LUPITA: No!

BORAT: What now?!

LUPITA: You don't have a condom, Steve.

BORAT: You don't have one?

LUPITA: I'm not the kinda girl who carries condoms in her purse.

BORAT: Well, you should.

LUPITA: And I don't want to sleep with you.

BORAT: C'mon, Lupi! It's been a month since we started dating.

LUPITA: Rides home in your cab doesn't really translate as "dating".

BORAT *(trying to kiss her):* How does this translate?

LUPITA *(stopping him):* Your name is not Steve.

BORAT: What are you talking about?

LUPITA: I can tell. The name Steve doesn't mean anything to you. All men react to their own names whispered in their ears when they're making out. You don't even hear it. "Steve" doesn't ring any bell to you.

BORAT: What bell? What difference does it make?

LUPITA: Like between a lie and the truth?

BORAT: I love you, that's the truth.

LUPITA: All right...

BORAT: You deserve the best, Lupi. I wish I had money to buy you a ring with diamonds and...

LUPITA: Stop! Not an extra word!

BORAT: OK... my name is not Steve. But ...

LUPITA: You know what. I actually know who you are. You're another horny immigrant with no papers. You don't react to the name Steve but your hand is shaking each time a cop passes by. This is not your cab. You're illegal and desperate. No, not ONLY to get laid. To find someone with a green card to marry you.

BORAT: Why do you have to spoil this?

LUPITA: And I bet you've never even been to Tennessee.

BORAT: We can go there together! On honey-moon.

She opens the car's door.

LUPITA: I'm done here. I'm gonna take another cab.

BORAT: Listen, Lupita! My real name is Borat.

LUPITA *(getting out of the car)*: Ha, ha! Not funny.

BORAT: Wait! That was not a joke!

He runs after her. He stops her.

BORAT: I'm telling you the truth. That "Borat" movie star ruined my life, I can't tell anyone my real name is Borat, they laugh at me. You laughed too!

LUPITA: And you don't have papers. That's why you lied.

BORAT: Well… Yes. That too.

LUPITA: OK. Let's say I understand that. I've been there.

BORAT: Good. So we are OK now? (*He attempts to kiss her.*)

LUPITA (*rejecting him*): Wow. Take it easy. I need to process all the info. Then make a decision.

BORAT: OK. Sorry. I just … I really like you. I do.

LUPITA: What exactly do you like about me?

BORAT: You are sexy. Beautiful! Smart. Nice. I dunno… I just like you.

LUPITA: And what do you want from me?

BORAT: I want to drive you home every night. Like we did. To talk about your clients, about my clients. (*he tries to make her laugh*) About all those rich fuckups and their little penises…

LUPITA: Don't try to sweet talk your way out of my question. What do you want from me?

BORAT: I want to… sit on a couch together, drinking vodka, watching TV … Making out... Making love… A LOT. Until we're dizzy-dizzy but good-dizzy-dizzy. I just want to love you. To spend the rest of my life with you.

LUPITA: And what role does the green card play in all that? What does it come first: green card or love?

BORAT: That's an impossible question. Life is not black and white. Or first - black and second - white. There's a whole rainbow out there.

LUPITA: Green card or love, Borat?

BORAT: Both. It's both. Knowing that you had a green card helped …

LUPITA: Of course.

BORAT: It did help me… It helped me to go on with liking you. To believe that we have a future together. That is something possible. Practical. Real. To love you, I mean.

SCENE 13 / DREAMSCAPE IV

Friday night, around 2 am. Nadia is on the street, waving to cabs. She's barefoot and disheveled. She throws up.

NADIA: Cab! Cab! *(beat)* What do you mean – "I do only Manhattan"? Washington Heights is in Manhattan!

Nadia is crying. She sees a public phone. She staggers to it. She dials.

NADIA: Borat? Answer, please! Borat?! … Please, please … Answer!

She waits for many seconds before hanging up. She stares at the audience. She dials again.

NADIA: C'mon, Borat! Where are you, where the fuck are you?

(She hears a POLICE CAR)

She runs away from the phone and hides.

Reality is getting blurred. INS 1 and INS 2 appear out of nowhere.

Nadia tries to toughen up, to face them.

NADIA: What?!… I did it…. Yes… I went to a veeeery cool party. In Soho. Wall Street guys. Yes, fancy! All in expensive suits. And the women – in designer clothes, yes, like in "Sex and the City"! Perfect teeth. Perfect hair. Elegant. Stylish. Friendly. What?! I know I'm not one of them! I went there to work! To ENTERTAIN. I am a clown artist! I am somebody! What?! *(pause)* Everybody was… laughing, drinking, smoking… I learned new words in English: ganga, weed, pot, grass. Yes, drugs! They were smoking drugs, they were cool.

INS 1 / INS 2: Drugs?!

INS 1: You used drugs.

INS 2: And you're proud of it.

NADIA: I didn't know much about drugs. Mike noticed and laughed, he said: "she's a drug virgin".

INS 1: Who's "Mike"?

INS 2: Mr Big?

NADIA: Let me explain…. I get there …. I am soooo excited… My heart is pumping hot steams not blood… This guy Mike ushers me in. He is confident, elegant. He says: "Hi, pretty lady." He takes my arm. He introduces me to people. He tells them: "She's from the former Soviet Union". He prepares a drink for me. A cocktail. A Cosmo! Yeah… I drink, I smoke, like everybody else… I am cool… I dance for him, for them… I am sexy, I shake it well!… A few hours pass, I think… I get tired… My stomach is a bit upset…. But it doesn't matter, everything is too perfect… I walk into this room… Beautiful room… A bedroom with red-painted walls and huge windows... I can see the Hudson River… great view!… Red lights dancing on the river … I press my face on that window… My feet hurt from dancing two hours on spike heels… I take off my shoes for a moment. Just for a moment. I think I'm alone. I am not alone. Mike enters. He comes closer… I can smell his expensive aftershave… He's gonna kiss me! No. He puts his hand under my skirt… Strange… His face looks different… "Say something in Russian, Natasha!" He keeps calling me Natasha... "You, Russian babes, are all so fucking sexy" ... What is he doing?... His hand... His fingers... Pushing my underwear, pushing... "C'mon, Natasha! Say FUCK ME, Mike, in Russian, Natasha!" ... *(pause)*

I keep staring at those red lights dancing in the river... like mouths with blood-red lips, laughing in the river ... while they... how many are they? .... I think 4 or 5 ... I stop counting after a while, I just stare at those mouths laughing in the river... and they are... you know, fucking me... riding me... I don't see their faces... I can't feel anything... I'm a dog balloon, flying... but I hear them: yeaaa, Nataaaaasha...

I'm trying to yell at them "my name is Nadia, motherfuckers!" and all the curses I know, spring out of me, in Russian! ... But the words can't actually get out of me. They just can't... And they're laughing and laughing ... no, not because I am a good clown...

(pause)

I had to run barefoot out of that room. Out of that apartment. Out… and I left them there… I left my shoes… I didn't have time to grab my Manolo Blahniks… Lupita will kill me … and that's fine with me … that's fine… I deserve that. *(she sees a CAB)* Hey, cab, cab, please stop, stop, please stop! I wanna go home. Home.

She tries to run. The INS guys stop her and "arrest" her.
They push her down the floor with the hands behind her back. She's defeated.

INS 1: We will send you home, Natasha

INS 2: Natasha

INS 1: Back to Moldova.

INS 2: Back home.

INS 1: She won't forgive you.

INS 2: You lost her shoes.

INS 1: She worked hard for those shoes.

INS 2: She was nice to you, and you were

INS 1 / INS 2: Irresponsible.

INS 1: Bad.

INS 2: Ungrateful.

INS 2 / INS 1: Wrong.

INS 1: You are done.

INS 2: There's nobody here to help you.

INS 1: Nobody cares for you.

INS 2: Nobody gives a shit.

INS 1 / INS 2: Nobody.

INS 2: They want you out.

INS 1: You're not a good friend.

INS 2: You're a Russian whore.

INS 1: You're an alien.

INS 1 / INS 2: ILLEGAL.

INS 2: You can't even go to the Police.

INS 1: You can't do anything.

INS 2: You're nobody.

INS 1: It's over.

INS 2: O-V-E-R.

INS 1 / INS 2: Over.

They laugh.

SCENE 14

Lupita's and Nadia's apartment.

Nadia sits on the sofa covered with a blanket. Her hair is wet like she just got out of the shower. She looks empty and emotionless.

Bob sits on the floor drinking shots of vodka. He looks worried and helpless.

Bottles of vodka and cans of beer surround him, as well as balloon animals.

Long pause.

BOB: C'mon, have a vodka shot!

Nadia shakes her head "no". She feels like puking at the sight of vodka.

Pause.

BOB: You gotta eat something. You puked the guts outta you. Wanna eat something? *(beat)* I can make spaghetti or... I dunno, I can make you a sandwich.

Nadia shakes her head violently "no". Pause.

BOB: I mean ... you know ... just tell me what you want...

Nadia doesn't look at him. Bob drinks another shot. Pause.

BOB *(exploding)*: That bitch, that fuckin' Lupita, what was in her freakin' mind to send you over there!?

NADIA: It's not her fault.

BOB: Right, not her fault! Stupid whore!

NADIA: She's not a whore. *(beat)* Her shoes, I lost her shoes...

BOB: Who cares about a freakin' pair of shoes when...*(you got abused)*!

Long pause. Vodka shot.

BOB: OK. We gotta do something about this ... We can't ... I mean we should report it to the Police.

NADIA *(suddenly alive, snapping at him)*: No police! Don't tell anyone about this! Anyone! Promise me you won't tell anyone! Promise!

BOB: OK. OK...

She starts destroying the balloon animals she finds under the sofa. She dismembers and tears them.

NADIA: Give me your word! Cross your heart!

BOB: OK, calm down! Easy, now, easy!

NADIA: Promise! Promise! Promise!

Bob immobilizes her, tenderly.

BOB: OK! I won't tell anyone.

Pause.

NADIA: Thanks.

She calms down and starts staring at the floor.

BOB: OK. We're OK.

Pause.

NADIA: Thank you. For getting me home.

BOB: It's good you didn't toss my number.

Pause.

NADIA *(matter-of-factly):* I want to disappear in that crack in the floor. I want to become liquid and pour myself out of me. Then evaporate.

Pause. Bob gulps down another shot of vodka.

BOB: You know, Ginger... It's hard, I know it's hard, yeah, I know how hard it is... *(beat)* Sometimes, you know, you see two roads: one nice and clear, the other one full of stones. And you choose the second. Why? Because, if you take the clear road, you'd always wonder about the stones on the other road. So you go for the stones and the hardships, and you know it was the wrong choice, but you did it, you put your head in the lion's mouth, like in a circus, but you did it in this big Circus called Life, yes, you put your head in the mouth of your fear, and yes, you got bitten, hard, very hard. BUT you still have your head, and you still have your eyes and you can see the ocean at the end of the road. And you don't regret not taking the first road, the one directly to the ocean, because you faced the lion, and you stepped on all those stones, and eventually you still got to the ocean... And you can tell your grandchildren: I did that. I walked on a difficult road and I survived. Your grandma Ginger was there and there and there, and now she is here, with you. Your grandma Ginger is... awesome.

Pause.

NADIA: My name is Nadia, not Ginger. Nadia is my real name. Nadia. Please say my name, Nadia. Nadia. I am Nadia. Nadia.

Bob goes to the sofa and sits next to her. He awkwardly puts his arms around her shoulders.

BOB: Nadia. What a beautiful name.

Nadia curls up in Bob's arms. They sit like that, glued to each other, in silence.

V – YOU MUST EAT

SCENE 15

Sunday morning. *Nadia sits on the sofa deadpan. Lupita comes from the kitchen with a bowl of cereals with milk.*

LUPITA: C'mon, you must eat something. They're Raisin Bran with fiber. Good for your body.

NADIA: No.

LUPITA: It's been more than / 36 hours …

NADIA: I can't.

Lupita tries to feed her like she'd do with a child, forcing the spoon inside her mouth.

LUPITA: You can.

NADIA: Leave me alone.

LUPITA: Sure. I left you alone two days ago and look what happened. *(she doesn't want to talk directly about the rape)* You lost my shoes.

NADIA: I will buy you new ones.

LUPITA: Right. Like you're a millionaire or something. *(mocking her)* "I'll buy you new ones". You don't even have money to pay the rent.

NADIA: Do you have to mention that now?

LUPITA: Yeah. Maybe that will move your ass out of that sofa. Out of that blanket wrapped around you like a fish tail… Who the hell do you think you are, the little mermaid?

NADIA: I can't move.

LUPITA: Listen, girl. We cried together, we felt sorry for ourselves, we spoke about how shitty this world is and how we, the immigrants, get shit everyday… Enough is enough. Thicken your skin. OK, you got raped, it's bad, it's very bad, it's fucking awful, but you're not dead, you're alive and you got stuff to do... (*matter-of-factly*) Do you have abdominal pain or hemorrhage?

NADIA: I don't think so.

LUPITA: You don't think so or you don't have?

NADIA: I don't have.

LUPITA: You took the "morning after" pill I gave you, right?

NADIA: Yes.

LUPITA: OK. We're fine. No shit will grow inside your womb. You're OK with that, aren't you? (*Nadia doesn't answer, any word about the rape hurts her*) I knew this girl, Lena, a Columbian chick, she got pregnant after a rape and kept the child. The kid is an American citizen coz he got born here, so she's happy now, she got her green card. But I don't think you wanted that kinda stuff, did you?

NADIA (*doesn't want to talk about the rape*): Can I have some cereals?

LUPITA: Finally.

*She hands Nadia the bowl, Nadia eats so she doesn't have
to talk.*

LUPITA: Honey… don't think I'm insensitive … I'm
not … but we must keep going, that's all. We can't
afford depressions and – how do they call it? – "post-
traumatic stress" and other shit like that. Only rich
people do. We can't afford to go to the shrink. We
can't afford / to … (waste time on post-traumatic
stress)

NADIA: I got your point. Please … (shut up)

Long pause.

LUPITA *(feeling guilty):* I'm gonna tell all the girls not
to trust that shit who talked me into that Soho-gig…
Criminal pigs, nobody will work for them anymore!

Pause.

NADIA: Can I pay the rent in a week or so?

LUPITA: You know what … no rent this month.
You're just a friend who stays with me. This month.

NADIA *(gratefully):* Thanks.

*She makes an effort and stands up. She walks. Lupita
laughs.*

LUPITA: Alleluia!

Nadia makes an easy clowning trick, but she staggers and falls. She makes a gesture towards Lupita – she doesn't want to be helped.

NADIA: And the little mermaid staggered and fell coz she wasn't used to walking, she never had legs before…

Nadia takes the balloon-dog and the balloon-squirrel from under the sofa and makes them enact the story she's telling to Lupita.

NADIA: One night, in the happy tree, the dog was sleeping and dreaming. An ugly worm came and ate the dog's wings: hup-hup-hup. The dog fell from the tree and got hurt. The squirrel woke up and rushed down the tree, to the dog. His eyes were closed, he was almost dead. "Please, dog, don't die! – said the squirrel. "Don't leave me alone, please!" The dog opens his eyes and smiles. "I can't be killed, squirrel. I have extraordinary skills. They knock me down, but I get up, again, and again, and again" He pushes himself hard and gets up. He staggers. He falls. He gets up again. "See, squirrel, nobody can stop me. Nobody can stop us."

SCENE 16

Two weeks later. Borat is driving, drinking vodka and talking on the phone.
Nadia is on her lunch break, in the backyard of a McDonalds.

BORAT: I mean, how long can I go like this? I still sleep on that freaking mattress on the Albanian's floor, all the money I make go home to mama, she needs to have heart surgery now, and at her age... I mean, yes, I should be there with her, but... What money can I make over there, Ginger?

NADIA: Nadia. I don't call myself Ginger anymore.

BORAT: Yeah, I gave up that Steve shit too. (*He gulps down a serious quantity of vodka.*)

NADIA: Look, Borat, I'm on my lunch break, you keep me on the phone on my lunch break. And you can't imagine how hungry you get when you're dressed like a cheeseburger. All you can think about is the moment you'll eat the real thing, I guess it's a sort of... revenge syndrome. (*Borat laughs*) It's not funny. Well, it is.

BORAT: So you're doing many clowning gigs these days?

NADIA: Yeah, everyday. I need to make money. They pay cash and don't ask for social security. All they wanna know is your first name. You could do that too.

BORAT: Naaah. It's not for me. But you sound good. You're doing well.

NADIA: Well... It's good to keep my mind busy, focused on work. I owe lots of money to Lupita.

BORAT(*singing*): Lu-pi-ta! Lu-pi-ta! Lu-pi-ta!

NADIA: Stop it, Borat! You sound like shit.

BORAT: There's something in your voice. Something different.

NADIA: It's... I dunno... (*she forces herself to speak about something nice, nothing about the rape, moving forward with a positive attitude*)

This guy Bob! ... he plays guitar and harmonica. We will try a duo. He is a musician. And he learned to make balloon animals!

BORAT: I could never learn to make those silly dogs.

NADIA: You didn't want to learn.

He drinks.

BORAT: Can I come visit you and Lupita? On Friday or maybe Saturday afternoon, before she goes to work.

NADIA: If Lupita doesn't want to see you, I can't invite you...

BORAT: Do you think she will get back to me?

NADIA: You didn't even tell me about the two of you. SHE told me. She's a good friend.

BORAT: She would be with me if I was American. We need to solve this papers thing...

NADIA: Maybe Bob could help. He got me this cell phone. Bob / is really... (a nice guy)

BORAT (*tipsy*): Bob this, Bob that, Bob super-that... You're lucky. (*he gulps vodka, with noise*) Weah!

NADIA: That vodka is gonna get you in trouble!

BORAT(*tipsy*): Yeah, sure, "mama".

Lights shift. Lupita is at home. She wears a house dress, NOT a sexy outfit. She looks at herself in the mirror.

LUPITA: You know what, Lupita honey, you look OK in a house dress. Not so glamorous, I give you that. But fine. Peaceful. Quite beautiful, actually. *(beat)* Yeah, I know, you can't be a star with babies clinging to your skirt, but hey. Look at Angelina Jolie! *(beat)* This guy, Borat. I dunno. It's not like he's a bad guy or something… He's OK … He's cute… He's genuine, real… Penniless, but real. I mean it's good to have money, but… I can hear grandma': "El dinero no compra felicidad… *(beat)*

He says he loves me… Is he really? … When you're desperate to get papers, you put your hopes around someone's neck and call it LOVE… I don't buy this thing with: "it's both!". He should have said: "Of course it's love. It's love!" If it IS love. I mean I want to be truly LOVED – actually ADORED - if I am to settle down for a loser like him… *(beat)* OK, let's see.

Can I picture you married with a cab driver? Can I see him in the living room, on the sofa? Can I see you next to him? Right. I can see two couch potatoes watching TV. Cracking jokes. Making love. And who's paying the rent?

(beat) I'm sorry, Lupita honey, this "role" is not for you. You gotta star in something else.

SCENE 17

That Sunday. Nadia, in the CHEESEBURGER costume and Bob, in a DIET COKE costume are on a short break, in the backyard of a McDonalds.

NADIA: You're good. You play the harmonica very well.

BOB: That was a surprise for me too. I haven't played in like... eight years.

NADIA: May I ask why?

BOB: Why what?

NADIA: You haven't played for so long.

BOB: My shrink said it was a masochistic act of rebellion against my wife in particular and my marriage in general.

NADIA: We were funny together. I mean with the gig. The kids laughed.

BOB (attempting a bow): I was just an accompaniment for the Cheeseburger "star" here.

NADIA (laughing): No. You were great!

BOB: No, YOU were great!

NADIA: YOU were great!

BOB: You were great!

NADIA: No, you!

BOB: We were great!

They laugh. They look at each other.

BOB: I guess it's funny to see a Diet Coke playing the harmonica, that's all.

NADIA: It's a good gig. $13/hour. Shall we do an extra hour?

BOB: It's up to you. I'm at your orders today.

NADIA: Are you tired?

BOB: I feel a bit ridiculous in this costume, but it also gives me some sorta perverse pleasure. I can't really define it. I guess it's good to not be sitting in a chair or on a sofa like I do every-fuckin'-day.

NADIA: So we stay longer, don't we?

BOB: Yeah. It's good to make money.

(he actually enjoys spending time with her)

NADIA: Yeah.

BOB: You're really funny. When you work.

NADIA: I am.

BOB: How come you're so funny?

NADIA: I'm a professional clown, it's my job to be funny.

BOB *(half-joking)*: You're not so funny in real life.

NADIA *(mockingly)*: Thanks.

BOB *(mockingly)*: You're welcome.

NADIA: I dunno, today I woke up in this great mood. It hasn't happened to me for so long. A mood like – everything is possible, Nadia! Yeah, I was really funny today. People laughed a lot. I'm not always that funny.

BOB: I was in a good mood too. I still am actually.

NADIA: It must be the sunny weather…

BOB: Definitely…

NADIA: It's a nice day…

Pause. They look at each other.

BOB: An imagination exercise.

NADIA: What?

BOB: Imagine a Diet Coke kissing a Cheeseburger.

(They both laugh.)

NADIA: Funny!

BOB: Can you picture it?

NADIA: You're not very subtle.

BOB: I can't be very subtle wearing this.

NADIA: Let's try.

BOB: What?

NADIA: To see if it's possible.

BOB: Kissing?

NADIA: Just as an exercise.

BOB: Right. To see if we can put imagination into practice.

NADIA: Yeah.

BOB: It'd be nice.

NADIA: Yes.

The DIET COKE tries to kiss the CHEESBURGER. It fails miserably.

They laugh.

NADIA: It doesn't work.

BOB: Apparently.

NADIA: But it was funny.

BOB: It was very funny. (*They laugh.*)

NADIA: We can do this trick in front of the kids. It can be very successful.

BOB: Well, I'm not so thrilled to repeat a failed kiss over and over again.

NADIA: Sorry. I always think of new tricks.

BOB: You should open a clowning business. Birthday parties and stuff. You can make a decent living from that.

NADIA: I don't think I can open a business. Yet. But I will. That's why I came here. I will open a clowning business, you're right. I only need to … solve some problems.

BOB: You don't have a greencard, do you.

NADIA: Yes. I mean, no. I don't.

BOB: That's a bummer.

NADIA: Yeah.

BOB: Well, I suspected something…(*joking*) You're dangerous!

NADIA (*sadly*): I got a deportation letter, Bob. I need to find a solution.

BOB: A deportation letter?

NADIA (*sadly*): I don't want to leave.

BOB: Don't make that face! We'll find a solution. Hey, Bobby-the-sad-clown-detector is here! He is here to make Nadia smile, to make Nadia happy. We don't like sad clowns! (*beat*) I won't let them deport you.

VI – LOVE & MARRIAGE

SCENE 18

Lupita is visiting Borat in prison. Long pause.

LUPITA: I don't know what to say.

BORAT: Thank you for coming. You're the only one /
who…

LUPITA: How could you be so fucking stupid? To
drink vodka and drive? When you don't even have a
driver's license?!

BORAT: They will deport me.

LUPITA: Of course.

BORAT: You don't care…

LUPITA: I moved my ass here! And it's not like I'm a
big fan of prisons…

BORAT: I'm sorry… Thank you.

Pause.

LUPITA: Nadia says hello. She and Bob / are…

BORAT: This Bob guy … is he serious?

LUPITA: They're like inseparable now. They even
work together. She turned the guy into a clown, can
you believe that?

BORAT: She must marry him.

LUPITA: Bob got her a lawyer. There are ways to
cancel the deportation. They need to get married and

prove that the marriage is real. That they are IN LOVE, that they got to know each other, spend time together… stuff like that. Which is true, they don't have to lie. I can testify those two fell in love in my living room.

BORAT: That's nice of you.

LUPITA: I can hire a lawyer for you.

BORAT: And… marry me?

LUPITA: (beat)I can't do that, Borat. I'm sorry.

BORAT: Then there's no point for a lawyer now. "Expedited removal". Tomorrow they send me home. And you know what – in a kinda weird way – I wanna go. Mama is on her way out. It's good to be there when she… you know, departs.

LUPITA: That's good then. You'll be with your mom.

Lupita doesn't know what else to say. Pause.

BORAT: I'd like to kiss you.

They can't do that there. She blows him a kiss. He "catches" it.

LUPITA: Kiss.

BORAT: Kiss.

The visit-is-over ring can be heard.

LUPITA: OK. I gotta go now.

BORAT: Kiss!

She starts to leave, trying to hide her tears.

BORAT: Hey, Lupi!

LUPITA: Yes.

BORAT: The green card doesn't matter. You matter.

LAST INS DREAMSCAPE

A few weeks later. *Nadia, in a clownish wedding gown, is alone on stage.*

Incision in her mind: *INS 1 and INS 2 are rapid-fire quizzing her.*

INS 1: Did you meet him in New York?

INS 2: Were you working under the table?

NADIA: Yes. No!

INS 1: So you dated intermittently in New York?

NADIA: Yes.

INS 2: So it's more like a business arrangement?

INS 1: For a green-card.

INS 2: US citizenship?

NADIA: No! It's not an arrangement.

INS 1: What did his parents say?

NADIA: They …

INS 2: What's his mother's maiden name?

INS 1: What's his mother's bra size?

INS 2: What's his grandmother's hobby?

INS 1: What's the name of his first pet?

NADIA: His…

INS 1: What's his favorite beer?

NADIA: Guinness!

INS 2: What's his favorite TV show?

INS 1: What toothpaste does he use?

INS 2: What deodorant?

INS 1: Does he eat hotdogs with mustard or ketchup?

INS 2: What salad dressing does he like?

INS 1 / INS 2: You don't know!

INS 1: Do you really know him?

INS 2: Have you ever met his mom?

INS 1: His dad?

INS 2: His sister?

INS 1: Have you ever met his sister's brother-in-law's mother?

INS 2: Have you ever met his sister's brother-in-law's mother-in-law?

NADIA: I don't....

INS 1: What elementary school did he go to?

INS 2: When did he have the first crush on a girl?

INS 1: Did the girl have braces?

INS 2: What was her bra size?

INS 1: When did he have sex for the first time?

INS 2: When did you two have sex for the first time?

NADIA: He... we ...

INS 1: When did he have his first erection?

INS 2: What was the ceremony actually like?

NADIA: The ceremony?

INS 1 / INS 2: The wedding!

INS 1: What did he say about your dress?

INS 2: When exactly did he say something about your dress?

INS 1: You didn't wear a dress?

INS 2: Pants?

INS 1: Pants!?

INS 2: Clown pants?

INS 1: Are you making fun of us?

INS 2: Is that a joke?

INS 1: A trick?

INS 2: Did you actually have a wedding?

INS 1: Do you actually have a husband?

INS 2: Where is your husband?

INS 1: What's his name?

INS 2: Your husband's name?

NADIA: I am not … I am not YET … I will… / I…

INS 1: Name!

INS 2: Name!

INS 1 / INS 2: Name! Name! Name!

NADIA: Bob! I am marrying Bob. I am. Don't you dare stop me!

Bob enters, dressed for the wedding.

Circus music combined with wedding music.

Nadia and Bob are dancing. Lupita enters.

Nadia, Bob and Lupita are addressing the audience and the INS guys.

NADIA: We did it!

BOB: We got married.

LUPITA: They did it. They got married.

NADIA: It feels strange.

BOB: But good.

NADIA: Very good.

LUPITA: After I visited Borat in prison, I told her: girl, you gotta solve this situation. The papers, I mean. The immigration guys know you and Borat worked together...

BOB: I didn't think I'd get married again but ... we had to solve her situation.

NADIA: I didn't want to get married for a green card.

LUPITA: But you like him, girl, you... (love him.)

NADIA: He makes me laugh.

BOB: She makes me laugh.

LUPITA: I said: guys, let's not overanalyze this. You gotta get married. And God knows, I'm not the kinda gal who preaches marriage but, in this case...

NADIA: He understands me.

BOB: It's kinda corny but ... she really gets me.

LUPITA: They were sitting on the sofa together, every freaking day. And he even stopped bringing beers. He'd play harmonica instead. And twist balloons. I had to get rid of them. "Go to Brighton fucking Beach – walk each other over there!"

NADIA: We take long walks together.

BOB: I took her to Brighton Beach.

LUPITA: I gave her an ultimatum: You get married or you are both outta here. I need my sofa back. You know, to find myself. I've been going through lots of shit lately.

NADIA: He makes perfect coffee.

BOB: I make shitty coffee but she likes it.

LUPITA: So yeah. I sent them to the City Hall. And I don't regret it.

BOB: She makes great burgers.

NADIA: I always burn the burgers, but he likes them.

LUPITA: As for me ... I'm taking an acting class! Only one course for now but I'll make more money and take two next semester. Marilyn Monroe, Al Pacino, De Niro – they all studied at my school.

NADIA: He talks in his sleep. I don't want to shake him, I just kiss him on the shoulder, and he turns towards me.

BOB: She daydreams a lot. I don't want to yell at her, to get her back to reality. I just kiss her on the neck. And she's there, with me, again.

LUPITA: Love. A funny little word.

NADIA: If this is a dream, I don't want to wake up.

BOB: This is not a dream. This is real.

Balloons and/or green cards start pouring from the ceiling, circus music.

EPILOGUE

Nadia has the dog balloon and the squirrel balloon and enacts the story.

NADIA: The dog and the squirrel got married and lived happily ever after. They are looking at the ocean from their home in Brighton Beach. They have dog-squirrel babies or puppies or puppirells or whatever you want to call them. They all have American wings now but they like to walk, in the evenings, with the whole family on the Russian promenade. Sometimes they stop and make tricks. Clown tricks. They are a family of clowns. They own a Birthday-Parties business! They have extraordinary skills in making people and animals laugh. They make people and animals happy. Woof-woof! Woof-woof! They are happy. They are.

INS 1 and INS 2 enter wearing scary-clown masks.

BLACKOUT

Notes on Contributors

JOHN CLINTON EISNER is Artistic Director of the Lark Play Development Center which he co-founded in 1994 as a community of theater professionals dedicated to the playwright's vision. He has built the Lark into an award-winning "think tank for the theater," with local, national and global reach, providing a creative community to thousands of participating playwrights, actors and directors, and a throng of community leaders, donors, volunteers and students. The company has hosted emerging and established artists from 48 different countries, supporting 130 playwrights last year alone. Over the past three years, Eisner worked with 30 partner institutions to advance 104 Lark-developed plays to 122 productions across the country and the world, and, in 2009, the company received an OBIE Award Grant and a Lucille Lortel Award for "Outstanding Body of Work." Previously, Eisner worked as actor, director, administrator, and casting associate on and off Broadway and in regional theater. He is active as a consultant and currently sits on the Lucille Lortel Awards Committee, advisory boards of *TheatreForum* and Transport Group, and the National Theatre Conference, among others. Eisner grew up in Madison, Wisconsin, earned a BA from Amherst College and an MFA from the National Theatre Conservatory, and lives in New York City with his wife, actress Jennifer Dorr White, and two children, Hannah and Jake.

SAVIANA STANESCU (www.saviana.com) was born in Bucharest, Romania, on a cold February morning during Ceausescu's dictatorship, and "reborn" in New York in the hot days of 2001. Her plays have been widely presented internationally and in the US. Recent New York productions include 'Aliens with extraordinary skills" off-Broadway at Women's Project (published by Samuel French), "Waxing West" (2007 New York Innovative Theatre Award for

Outstanding Full-length Script) and "YokastaS Redux" at La MaMa Theatre, "Flag Stories" at TBG Theatre (part of Myth America Project, a collage of texts by Arthur Kopit, Theresa Rebeck, Israel Horowitz, Jason Grote, etc), "Suspendida" and "Vicious Dogs on Premises" (with Witness Relocation) at the Ontological Theatre, "Balkan Blues" at the NYC Fringe Festival, the E-Dating Project at Strasberg Institute for Theatre&Film, and the site-specific "I want what you have" at the World Financial Center.

Saviana won the 2007 Marulic Prize for Best European Radio-drama for "Bucharest Underground". In Stockholm, Sweden, her play "White Embers" produced by Dramalabbet made it in the TOP 3 of Best Plays in 2008.

Saviana has published books of poetry and drama including "Aliens With Extraordinary Skills", "Waxing West", "Google me!" (poetry), "Black Milk" (four plays) and "The Inflatable Apocalypse" (Best

Romanian Play of the Year UNITER Award in 2000).

Other published work includes: monologues and

scenes in Smith&Kraus' annual anthologies,

"Aurolac Blues," performed at HERE Arts Center, in

the anthology "Plays and Playwrights 2006"; two

monologues in the Playwrights' Center's

"Monologues for Women", "Jelly-Love and Peanut-

Butter" in the "Estrogenius" anthology of new plays

by women.

"Final Countdown" was translated, produced and

published in France by Maison d'Orient, and "Lenin's

Shoe" was published by Fisher Verlag in the

anthology "Voices From undergroundzero New

York" in Germany.

Saviana's plays have received readings and

workshops at Long Wharf Theatre, New York Theatre

Workshop, Lark Play Development Center, New York

Stage&Film, Baryshnikov Arts Center, Playwrights'

Foundation, Traveling Jewish Theatre, Immigrants

Theatre Project, LaGuardia Performing Arts Center, Origin Theatre Company, etc.

Saviana was a 2005-2007 TCG fellow with the Lark Play Development Center, where her plays "Waxing West" and "Lenin's Shoe" had barebones productions. She also was a 2007-2008 NYSCA playwright-in-residence with Women's Project and writer-in-residence for Richard Schechner's East Coast Artists. She holds an MA in Performance Studies (Fulbright fellow) and an MFA in Dramatic Writing (John Golden Award for excellence in playwriting) from New York University, Tisch School of the Arts, where she now teaches in the Drama Department.

More titles from NoPassport Press

Antigone Project: A Play in Five Parts

by Tanya Barfield, Karen Hartman, Chiori Miyagawa, Lynn Nottage and Caridad Svich, with preface by Lisa Schlesinger, introduction by Marianne McDonald; **ISBN 978-0-578-03150-7**

Amparo Garcia-Crow: The South Texas Plays

(Cocks Have Claws and Wings to Fly, Under a Western Sky, The Faraway Nearby, Esmeralda Blue) **Preface by Octavio Solis;** ISBN: **978-0-578-01913-0**

Anne Garcia-Romero: Collected Plays

(Earthquake Chica, Santa Concepcion, Mary Peabody in Cuba)

Preface by Juliette Carrillo; ISBN: **978-0-6151-8888-1**

John Jesurun: Deep Sleep, White Water, Black Maria –

A Media Trilogy **Preface by Fiona Templeton; ISBN: 978-0-578-02602-2**

Lorca: Six Major Plays

(Blood Wedding, Dona Rosita, The House of Bernarda Alba, The Public, The Shoemaker's Prodigious Wife, Yerma) **In new translations by Caridad Svich, Preface by James Leverett, introduction by Amy Rogoway; ISBN: 978-0-578-00221-7**

Matthew Maguire: Three Plays

(The Tower, Luscious Music, The Desert) **Preface by Naomi Wallace; ISBN: 978-0-578-00856-1**

Oliver Mayer: Collected Plays

(Conjunto, Joe Louis Blues, Ragged Time) **Preface by Luis Alfaro, Introduction by Jon D. Rossini; ISBN: 978-0-6151-8370-1**

Alejandro Morales: Collected Plays

(expat/inferno, marea, Sebastian); **ISBN: 978-0-6151-8621-4**

12 Ophelias (a play with broken songs) by Caridad Svich
ISBN: 978-0-6152-4918-6

NoPassport is a sponsored project of Fractured Atlas, a non-profit arts service organization. Contributions in behalf of [Caridad Svich & NoPassport] may be made payable to Fractured Atlas and are tax-deductible to the extent permitted by law. **For online donations go directly to** https://www.fracturedatlas.org/donate/2623

www.ingramcontent.com/pod-product-compliance
Lightning Source LLC
Chambersburg PA
CBHW020638030726
47498CB00002B/263